THE VAMPIRE FATE

DARK WORLD: THE VAMPIRE WISH 4

MICHELLE MADOW

DREAMSCAPE PUBLISHING

1

ANNIKA

"Take me to the Haven," I commanded Geneva.

Going to the Haven was my only option.

When the vampire queen Laila of the Vale had handed me her stake and dared me to try to kill her, she clearly hadn't expected that I'd be able to do it.

I hadn't thought I'd been able to do it.

But that was why I'd disguised myself as a vampire princess and come to the Vale—to kill the vampire queen. And I'd done it. I'd driven a stake—her *own* stake—straight through her heart.

All that remained of the centuries old queen was a pile of ashes by my feet.

But I wasn't looking at Laila's remains after reaching for Geneva's sapphire ring and commanding her to take me to the Haven.

I was looking at Prince Jacen's silver eyes. The eyes currently staring at me with a mix of shock and anguish.

I couldn't blame him for looking at me like that. For weeks, he'd thought I was dead.

I'd thought he didn't care that I was dead. I'd thought he'd eventually planned on killing me himself. And I had a valid reason for thinking that, since it was what he'd told Queen Laila and the witch who acted as her second-in-command, Camelia. I'd seen the entire thing myself.

Jacen had no idea that I'd been masquerading around the palace in disguise, passing myself off as a mysterious vampire princess named Ana who had come to the Vale to seek his hand in marriage.

It had only been last night, during a private dinner with the prince, when I'd found out the truth. Jacen had *never* wanted me dead. Far from it.

He apparently hadn't been able to stop thinking about me since the last time we'd seen each other. Not only that, but he had his own plans of vengeance against the Vale—just like I did.

We were on the same side.

I was *so close* to coming clean with him last night about who I truly was. But I'd been scared. I thought that if I told him the truth, he would be furious and unable to forgive me.

But I couldn't keep lying to him. So that morning, I'd decided to tell him the truth.

I'd been about to do so when vampire guards had surrounded me and dragged me to the throne room where Queen Laila, Prince Jacen, Princess Karina, and the witch Camelia were waiting.

Somehow, Camelia had found out everything. She'd injected me with the antidote to the transformation potion I'd taken and revealed who I truly was—not Princess Ana from the Seventh Kingdom, but Annika, a human blood slave of the Vale. Not only that, but she knew I had Geneva's sapphire ring.

Luckily, she'd assumed I was hiding the ring in my quarters. She didn't know I was keeping it in a hidden pocket in my underwear.

She'd sent guards to my quarters to find the ring, but it wouldn't be long until they realized it wasn't there, and that they should check me more thoroughly.

Everyone was so shocked by Laila's death that I'd taken the moment for what it was—an opportunity to reach for the ring and command Geneva to transport me to the only place that *might* keep me safe—the kingdom of the Haven.

From what I knew about the Haven, it got its name because it was a safe haven for supernaturals. The vampires who lived there survived on animal blood, not human blood. But mostly, the Haven was neutral territory that believed in peace amongst all the kingdoms.

I just had to pray that once they heard my side of the story, they would help me.

Geneva was bound to do as I said, since I was the current owner of the sapphire ring that held her captive. So right after giving her the command, we both flashed out of the Vale.

I'd done what I'd come to the Vale to do—I'd killed Queen Laila.

My only regret was that I might never be able to come clean to Jacen with the truth.

2

ANNIKA

My stomach dropped, and I was surrounded by darkness.

Seconds later, my feet hit the ground, warmth surrounded me, and my vision came into focus.

I was standing in a courtyard. Full trees arched overhead, and while it was still dark, it had the feeling of right before sunrise. The entire place was *alive*—with greenery, chirping birds, and with vampires dressed in all white. They looked like they were at a yoga retreat—not like they lived in one of the most powerful kingdoms in the entire world.

The vampires were doing all sorts of things—sweeping, cleaning, and carrying baskets through the open halls.

Suddenly, they stopped what they were doing and

turned to me, their fangs out as they barreled in my direction.

"Protect me!" I called to Geneva.

The witch looked as shell-shocked as I felt as she held out her hands and spoke a spell.

I held my stake in front of me and bent my knees, ready to defend myself against the oncoming vampires.

Well, it wasn't really *my* stake. It was Laila's stake—the stake she'd handed me before challenging me to kill her.

When I'd killed her, the stake had done something to me. I'd felt a burst of warmth, and suddenly, my senses were as strong as they'd been while I was masquerading as a vampire.

But there was more to it than that. Because my reflexes had improved, too.

Out of nowhere, I'd known how to fight. I'd taken down the three vampire guards surrounding me as if it were nothing. And those vampires were *strong*. I shouldn't have been able to do that—not even after consuming vampire blood to temporarily give me the abilities of a vampire.

Except that the antidote Camelia had injected me with had *removed* the vampire blood from my system. When I'd staked Laila, it had been as a human.

I had no idea what had happened, but I knew one thing—I wasn't letting go of this stake.

Geneva was fast in casting her spell, and the oncoming vampires crashed into the barrier she'd erected around us. Their fangs were out and ready, their eyes savage as they tried to claw their way through.

"Why are they attacking?" I asked, glancing over at the witch. "I thought the vampires here didn't feed on humans?"

Geneva just crossed her arms, glaring at me and saying nothing.

This certainly wasn't the first time she'd looked at me with disdain or irritation—the witch clearly thought she was better than humans—but something about the way she was looking at me now was different.

She was staring at me with pure, undisguised *hate*.

"Answer me!" I yelled, somehow keeping my focus on both her and the mob of surrounding vampires, which was getting larger by the second. "I command you to answer my question."

"I can't say with certainty." She flipped her hair over her shoulder, refusing to look at me.

Great.

I studied the crowd, relieved when a statuesque vampire who appeared in control of herself made her way through. She wore the same thing as the others—a flowing, comfortable looking garment of all white—and her hair was in a braided crown that made her look like an ancient goddess.

She pushed past the rabid vampires, and it wasn't long until she reached us.

"The vampires here are not accustomed to being around humans," the mystery woman said, her cool gaze on me as she spoke. "You'd best tell Geneva to add a scent barrier to the boundary as well."

"Do as she said," I told Geneva. "Add a scent barrier to the boundary."

She must have obeyed, because a second later, the vampires stopped hissing and pounding against the boundary.

"Go," the woman told the vampires, her strong voice carrying through the courtyard. "Don't you all have chores to attend to before the sun rises?"

They lowered their eyes and shuffled away, picking up the various cleaning objects and baskets they'd discarded in the frenzy. Some of the objects had been destroyed—trampled on—and their owners hurried away with them, ducking their heads in shame.

It was only once they'd returned to their work that I felt it was okay to speak.

"The two of you know each other?" My gaze went back and forth between Geneva and the mystery woman. I eventually settled on focusing on the mystery woman, since Geneva seemed intent to look anywhere but at me.

I wasn't sure what I'd done to the witch, but whatever it was had clearly pissed her off.

"Geneva was a great asset to the vampires during the Great War," the woman said, clasping her hands together as she spoke. "The Haven, of course, stayed out of the fighting, but we fostered trust between the vampire kingdoms so they could work together to defeat our common enemy. However, we're getting ahead of ourselves, since I don't believe we've been officially introduced. I'm Mary—the leader of the Haven."

"You're an original vampire?" I asked, instantly wary. I hadn't thought of it while deciding to come here—I'd only had a few seconds to decide where to go at all—but an original vampire might not take too kindly to the fact that I'd just killed Laila.

"I am." She nodded. "And you are…?"

"Sorry." I pulled my stake back, realizing that not only had I not yet introduced myself, but that I was pointing a stake at her chest. "I'm Annika."

"You're a Nephilim," Mary said simply.

"What?" I'd heard Camelia say that word—Nephilim—after I'd killed Laila, but I'd been so consumed with trying to escape that I hadn't given it much thought.

"Your eyes have rings of gold around their pupils," she said. "The mark of the Nephilim."

"They don't," I said. "My eyes are brown."

I'd always wanted prettier eyes—green or blue—but I knew more than anyone that my eyes were a dull shade of chocolate brown.

"You must have come to your powers recently, then." Mary glanced at the stake in my hand, wariness crossing her features.

"She did." Geneva focused intently on Mary as she spoke. "She came into her powers when she killed Queen Laila."

3

ANNIKA

CRAP. There went any hope of keeping it secret from Mary that I'd killed one of her fellow original vampires.

"Stop." I glared at Geneva, wanting nothing more than to jam this stake through *her* heart. But of course, I held back. Geneva and I might not be the best of friends, but she'd helped me get this far—and I had no interest in committing cold-blooded murder. At least, not again. "I can speak for myself."

Geneva narrowed her eyes at me, full of absolute loathing.

I wasn't sure what I'd done to her between last time we'd spoken and now, but something between us had *clearly* changed. I'd have to work it out with her later. For now, she *had* to obey my command, since I controlled her ring.

"It's true, then." Mary said it to me as a statement, not a question. "You killed Queen Laila."

"I didn't mean to," I said, begging her to believe me. "Well, I *did* mean to, but she didn't give me much of a choice. It was her or me. I had to do it. Otherwise, I was as good as dead."

Geneva clenched her fists by her side, her lips pressed together. She looked like she was dying to contradict me.

I couldn't blame her. Because while what I'd said hadn't been a lie, I *had* gone to the Vale with the goal of killing the vampire queen.

"It seems we have much to discuss," Mary said after a few seconds of silence. "Come. Let's go to my cabin, where we can speak privately."

She turned around and led the way.

Geneva kept the boundary up around us as we followed Mary, which stopped the vampires from trying to attack again. In fact, they barely glanced at us as they went about their chores.

The way they calmly performed their tasks in their all white outfits was similar to how I imagined a commune.

Or a cult.

But as I followed Mary down the open hall, I was barely able to take in the exotic scenery of the Indian mountainside retreat. Because everything that had happened this morning at the Vale was finally starting to set in.

I'd killed not just Laila, but three of her guards.

I'd seen death before, yes. And I'd certainly fantasized about killing the vampires who had killed my family.

But seeing death and doing the killing were two completely different things.

I'd taken lives this morning. Four of them.

That was something I was going to have to live with forever.

It wasn't Laila I felt guilty about. After all, the vampire queen had founded the kingdom that had killed so many innocent humans and turned so many unwilling humans into vampires.

Killing her had saved so many future lives.

No—it wasn't Laila's death that plagued my mind. It was the guards.

I was glad that my guard Tess hadn't been one of the guards who had dragged me to the throne room—I never would have been able to hurt her—but I knew nothing about the guards who did. Many of the vampires in the

Vale had been turned against their will, like Jacen had been. They didn't *want* to be what they were. Yes, they'd likely killed before, but all vampires of the Vale had control of their bloodlust. They were killed otherwise—vampires who couldn't control their bloodlust were considered too much of a liability to live in the Vale.

The guards I'd killed probably had wives who loved them—perhaps they even had families. By dragging me to the throne room to face the royal vampires, they were only doing their job. They didn't deserve to die for that.

But if I hadn't killed them, they would have killed me first.

No matter what, I couldn't let myself forget that.

"We're here," Mary said as we approached a modern cabin. It was small and simple, surrounded by many other identical cabins.

"This is yours?" I asked. She'd said she was taking me to her cabin, but I'd expected the leader of the Haven to have a mansion—not a cabin the same size as all the others in the kingdom.

"It is." She nodded. "Here in the Haven, we believe in peace and equality. I'm not entitled to any more personal living space than anyone else."

"Does everyone here live alone?" I asked.

"No." She smiled. "There are other, larger cabins on

the other side of the community for citizens who choose to share their housing. The space is, of course, divided equally in accordance to the number of individuals inside the residence."

She was leading the way up the steps when something turned the corner of the cabin—a tiger.

Its eyes locked on mine, and I froze. It was huge—larger than I'd ever imagined a tiger could be—and it watched me with fierce intelligence. I couldn't move, afraid that one single motion would send it pouncing.

I'd heard about the Haven's legendary tiger shifters, but it was completely different seeing one in person.

"There's no need to fear the tigers," Mary said, as calm as ever. "They protect us. As long as you adhere to the Haven's law against violence while on our land, the tigers will protect you as well."

"Okay," I said, trying to ignore the way my hands itched for my stake. "Good to know."

The tiger yawned, and while the motion was harmless, I couldn't help but wonder if it was an excuse for it to show off its massive teeth.

Mary stepped up to the front door, pressed her finger against a panel, and it clicked open. "Come inside," she said, holding the door open for Geneva and me. "As I said before, we have much to discuss."

I scurried past the tiger, keeping my eyes on it the entire time, and followed her inside.

4

JACEN

THE THRONE ROOM had erupted into chaos.

Karina had gracefully stepped out of a side entrance soon after Annika and Geneva had disappeared. Camelia knelt down next to the pile of ashes, as if praying for Laila to rise. The three fallen guards lay dead beside her.

A few more guards had entered the room soon after Annika and Geneva had flashed out—the same guards who had been sent to Annika's quarters to find the sapphire ring. They'd informed me of what I already knew—the ring wasn't there.

Now the guards stared at Camelia hovering over the pile of ash, while others talked amongst themselves.

My mind whirred with everything that had just

happened, but I still caught snippets of their conversations.

"She can't truly be dead."

"The human killed the queen and three of the strongest guards."

"The queen will rise from the ashes."

"Death is coming to the Vale—we need to get out while we still can."

I couldn't say what was right and what was wrong. But I knew one thing—what had just happened couldn't get out to the public. If it did, everything would be a bigger mess than it already was.

"No one is to go anywhere." My voice boomed throughout the room, and I threw some compulsion into my tone, wanting to make sure they obeyed me. "You're all to stay in this room until I issue a further command."

The guards all straightened to attention, their eyes on me.

There wasn't much I liked about being a vampire—I hated pretty much every part of it. But compulsion definitely had its benefits.

Now, everyone was looking to me for instructions on what to do next. But my thoughts were consumed with only one thing.

Annika was alive.

I'd been beating myself up about her death since her corpse had been presented to me earlier this month. Now, I'd found out that not only was she alive, but she'd been here, in the palace—parading around as Princess Ana of the Seventh Kingdom.

I'd noticed that Princess Ana had mannerisms similar to Annika's, and I'd known there was something familiar about her when I'd kissed her. But I'd thought I was searching for reminders of the girl I'd lost before having a chance to explore what existed between us. I'd even thought it might be a sign that I was meant to choose Princess Ana to be my bride.

Then I'd chalked it up to my imagination. After all, I'd seen Annika's corpse. She was *dead*. No amount of wishful thinking was going to get her back.

Except that she wasn't dead. She'd lied to me and deceived me.

I understood her lying to everyone else in the court, but we'd been alone together numerous times. She'd had multiple chances to tell me the truth.

But she hadn't.

And I had no idea why not.

"Your Highness?" One of the larger guards stepped forward, his eyes on me. "What would you like us to do?"

"Stay where you are," I said, and I walked down the

steps to stand next to Camelia, who was still kneeling by the ashes. "How is Laila dead?" I asked the witch. "The queen herself said that only a Nephilim can kill an original vampire. The Nephilim are extinct. Yet, here we are." I motioned to Laila's ashes to show what I meant.

Camelia stood and faced me, her eyes wide with shock. "Annika *is* a Nephilim," she said, her voice smaller than I'd ever heard it before.

"She's not," I said, since I *knew* Annika. "She's human."

I thought back to the time I'd spent with her in the village—when I'd passed myself off as a human blood slave as an escape from life in the palace. Annika was definitely a human. Firstly, her blood smelled human. Secondly, and most importantly, she'd told me about how much she *hated* being human. Being human made her feel helpless. In fact, she'd wanted to be a vampire, so she could have the strength to fight back against anyone who tried to hurt her.

"She wasn't a human," Camelia said, her expression hard with conviction. "Right after she killed Laila, I looked into her eyes and saw the mark of the Nephilim."

That triggered a memory—something I'd read in the numerous encyclopedic volumes within the palace library. There wasn't much written about the Nephilim —the children of angels were extremely secretive, and vampires didn't know much about their race. But there was one big thing that all supernaturals knew about the Nephilim—they all had marks around their eyes. Golden rings around their pupils.

In the last moment before flashing out of the Vale, Annika had looked straight at me.

Her eyes had the marks. They'd never had them before, but they had them then.

"How is this possible?" I asked. "The Nephilim are extinct."

"They're supposed to be." Camelia glanced again at the spot where Annika had been standing before disappearing. "But Annika was very much alive, and as long as she remains that way, she's a threat to all supernaturals on Earth. She commanded Geneva to take her to the Haven. We *must* storm the Haven at once so we can kill Annika and acquire Geneva's sapphire ring."

"No." The word escaped my lips before I could think to stop it.

"Why not?" Camelia narrowed her eyes at me, tilting her head in question. "You don't still care about the girl, do you?" Her voice was controlled and threatening.

"Absolutely not." I straightened, knowing that I needed to play this right if I wanted to keep Annika as safe as possible. Because while I didn't know much about her—apparently much less than I'd ever thought, given that she was Nephilim and not human—I couldn't bear the thought of having her killed.

She was good. I knew it from the conversations I'd had with her as Annika *and* as Princess Ana. She wanted the same things that I did—rights for the humans of the Vale, and rights for humans to be able to have a choice on being turned.

Not only that, but there was an undeniable connection between us.

She cared about me, just as I cared for her. She might have lied about a lot, but I believed her feelings were real. If they hadn't been…

I shook it off, not wanting to let myself think that way.

I just needed to find out the truth, and I couldn't do that if she were killed. I also couldn't do that if the Vale thought I was on her side. If they thought I cared about a Nephilim, I would surely be hunted down and killed.

I needed to play my cards right if I wanted us to both make it out of this alive.

"The Haven is a safe haven," I reminded not just Camelia, but everyone else in the room. "Violence is not allowed on their lands. If anyone tries to attack Annika while she's in the Haven, the tiger shifters will pounce and kill them. And with the growing threat of the wolves outside our borders, the loss of any more of our men is the last thing we need."

The guards remained silent during this entire conversation—as expected, my compulsion had a strong hold on them.

"But will the Haven protect the Nephilim?" Camelia asked. "The Nephilim never cared that the Haven wanted peace—they believed *all* supernaturals should die. The citizens of the Haven didn't fight in the Great War, but they were a major influence in creating peace between the supernatural kingdoms so we could successfully band together to defeat the Nephilim. The Haven didn't want the Nephilim hunting supernaturals any more than we did. There's no saying *what* they'll do to a Nephilim who transports straight into their territory."

"There's only one way for me to find out," I said.

"And what way is that?" Camelia asked.

"By going there myself."

5

JACEN

"Alone?" Camelia looked at me like I was crazy. "That would be careless. You'll need backup."

"If I'm going to the Haven to lure Annika to leave of her own free will, sending backup would be callous," I countered, using her own language against her. "Annika already doesn't trust the Vale. If I came with backup, it would only put her more on guard than she already is."

"I don't think you realize how dangerous the Nephilim truly are," Camelia said. "Or did you already forget how easily she killed our queen and three of our strongest guards?"

"Of course I didn't forget." I scoffed, since it had happened only moments ago. "But I don't think *you* realize that Annika has a weak spot—for me. She disguised herself as a vampire princess and tried to marry me. Clearly, she's interested."

"She disguised herself as a vampire princess as a ploy to kill the queen." Camelia sneered.

"She did." I nodded. "But her feelings for me are real. If there's anyone who can loosen her up and convince her to leave the Haven, it's me."

"She's a con artist." Camelia crossed her arms, looking like a toddler who'd been denied her favorite toy. I wouldn't have been surprised if she'd stomped her foot as well. "You can't believe anything she said or did while here."

I turned to the guards. There were five of them in all, and they stood alert and ready, waiting for a command. "You all saw the way she looked at me," I told them, adding in a conceited smirk for good measure. "Was it or was it not the way a woman looks at a man when she's already half in love with him?"

I wasn't proud of the words—I knew how arrogant I sounded. But before being turned into a vampire prince, I'd been a well-known athlete on my way to the Olympics. I'd competed in major cities all over the world, hitting up bars with my team members where we'd been surrounded by adoring fans. I certainly wasn't inexperienced or unknowledgeable when it came to women. Quite the opposite, actually.

I needed to harness as much of that arrogance as I could if I wanted to convince Camelia to go along with my plan.

"I agree with the prince." Thomas, the highest in command of the guards in the room, stepped up and faced Camelia. "During the selection, the princess—I mean, the *Nephilim*—looked at Prince Jacen the way he claims she did."

"She was *acting*," Camelia hissed. "She *had* to pretend she cared for the prince if she intended on remaining in the palace."

"What about her final moments here?" I asked. "Her deception had been revealed—there was no need for her to act anymore. Yet, before she flashed out with Geneva, it was *me* she looked at with her heart in her eyes. You were standing near her—I know you saw it, too."

The guards were silent as they waited for Camelia's reaction. A few of them nodded in agreement to my statement.

"Perhaps," Camelia said, her fingers twisting around the wormwood pendant she always wore around her neck. "But she's a Nephilim. Her kind kills supernaturals—they certainly don't *love* them." She said the last part in disgust—as if a Nephilim and a vampire falling in love was the most heinous act ever.

"We all know that Nephilim are killers," I said, since if I wanted to gain their trust, I had to be convincing. "That bitch just killed our queen, and she used *my* selection to do it. She lied to me and played me for a fool. She needs to die for that. It's our job to see that done, and if she has a weakness for me, then I'm damned well going to exploit it. I'll trick her into trusting me, lure her away from the Haven, and kill her. A stake in the heart will be a deserving end after what she's done. Or do you not also want to avenge Queen Laila?" I stared at Camelia with fire in my eyes, daring her to go against me.

"Of course I want to avenge our queen." She dropped her hands to her sides, her eyes aflame. "But killing a Nephilim is far more difficult than you seem to realize. They're as fast as vampires, they're natural hunters, and they're immune to compulsion."

"Really?" I raised an eyebrow, since that explained how Annika had resisted my compulsion back when I'd tried to compel her to forget she'd ever met me. I'd assumed she was wearing wormwood—the only plant that when worn, could negate the effects of compulsion. She'd sworn she wasn't.

I supposed that was one time when she'd been telling the truth.

"Yes," Camelia answered. "Nephilim are the only

supernaturals who are immune to compulsion without the assistance of wormwood." She reached for the green pendant around her neck, as if to remind herself that her protection from compulsion was still there.

The witches of the Vale were the only ones in the kingdom permitted to wear wormwood. For all others, it was forbidden.

"She's also in control of Geneva's sapphire ring," Camelia reminded me. "You're one of the strongest vampires in the world, but even you're not strong enough to take down a Nephilim who has command over Geneva. *No* vampire could take her down alone—not even the originals themselves. What happened to our queen is proof enough."

"Our queen was caught off guard." I gazed solemnly at her ashes, as though pained by her death.

In reality, I couldn't be more thrilled that she was gone.

"Annika will be caught off guard as well." I ripped my gaze away from the ashes and clenched my fists to my sides, making sure to appear revved up and ready for revenge. "She might be a Nephilim, but she's also a woman. I'll tell her what I know she wants to hear—that I fell in love with her during the time we spent together in the palace, and that I'll do anything to be with her. I'll ask her to run away with me. Whatever it takes. Then, once we've crossed over the border of the Haven, my stake will be through her heart before she'll have time to touch the sapphire ring and beg the witch to save her."

"A decent plan," Camelia said. "But there's one major flaw in it."

"What's that?" I asked.

"You can't kill Annika while she's wearing the sapphire ring. We need that ring to protect the Vale. If she dies while wearing it, Geneva will die with her, and then we'll be at the mercy of the wolves without Geneva's help."

"Right," I said, having completely forgotten that small detail. "Perhaps you're right and I'll need backup. We'll station guards at an agreed meeting spot outside of the Haven."

"It's not a bad plan," Thomas said. "I believe we can work with this."

Camelia whipped her head around to glare at him. "Did the prince or I ask for your opinion?" she asked, eyes blazing.

"The guards are experienced fighters," I told the witch, and then I turned to face Thomas, dismissing her. "Please, continue."

"Thank you, Your Highness." He cleared his throat,

looking at me and not Camelia. "Your plan has a good chance of working, except that the Nephilim would surely catch our scent, which would ruin our element of surprise. But the wolves who attacked the Vale wore concealment charms that hid their scent from other supernaturals." He turned his gaze to meet Camelia's. "Can you create similar charms for us?"

"I cannot," Camelia said. "Those charms were created with dark magic. But Laila kept the charms that those wolves used, in case we had need of them again."

"Find them," he said. "Once you do, we can plan the specifics of the mission. If our prince truly has command over the Nephilim's heart—which I believe he does—then this might work."

"I'll find them," I promised. "I'll make sure of it."

Of course, I didn't intend on it getting that far. I had no idea what Annika's motivations were, but I didn't want her dead.

I just wanted to *talk* with her. We could do that safely in the Haven.

After all her lies, I wasn't sure if I could ever trust her again, but I needed to at least try to discover the truth. I knew she was Nephilim and that Nephilim hunted vampires, but I'd meant what I'd told Camelia and the guards—I believed her feelings for me were real. Her emotions had been plastered all over her face in those last few seconds when she'd looked at me. Pain, regret, and heartbreak.

That wasn't the look of someone who wanted me dead.

And while it would be all too easy to allow myself to be consumed with thoughts of Annika, I also needed to ensure that I kept my authority in the Vale. Because the wolves were coming—they were figuring out a way to get past our boundary, and the citizens of the Vale had no way of fighting them. The wolves had proven that when they'd attacked the town square. Yes, we had our guards, but they were far outnumbered by the wolves.

When I'd met with Noah—the First Prophet of the wolves—he'd told me all about how the wolves needed the vampires to leave the Vale so the wolves' Savior could rise. The wolves were determined to kill all the vampires to make that happen.

But there was another way. I could lead the vampires *out* of the Vale. When Noah had first proposed that idea, I'd thought it was ridiculous. Queen Laila would have never allowed it.

With Queen Laila dead, this was a new game entirely. I wasn't sure of the best way to play my cards yet, but given some time, I would figure it out.

Until then, I needed Camelia and the guards to believe I was on their side. Long-term thinking was crucial if I wanted myself, Annika, and the vampires of the Vale to get out of this alive.

The more trust I had, the more I could get away with when the time came to act.

"Very well," Camelia said. "In the meantime, it's the best interest of the Vale for us to not let anyone else know what happened today."

"How are we supposed to do that?" I pointed to the ashes. "Our queen is *gone*."

"And if the citizens of the Vale find out, there's no telling *what* they'll do," she said. "We must keep this secret until we establish a new chain of command. Your brothers can know, of course, but until we figure out how to spin this, the truth can't leave this room."

"Fine," I said, since with everything going on, it wasn't worth it for me to argue with her about this. To keep her placated, I faced the guards, pushing magic into my voice. "Until I say otherwise, you're to tell no one that Queen Laila is dead and that Princess Ana wasn't who she claimed to be," I said. "Understood?"

They all nodded, their faces slack from the effects of the compulsion, and said that they understood.

"Good," I said. "Now, clean up this mess and find Princess Karina. I need to make sure she knows the plan and follows it as well. In the meantime, I'm going to

Queen Laila's quarters to locate those concealment charms."

I stormed out of there, determined to find those charms.

Once I did, I would be one step closer to learning the truth about Annika's intentions once and for all.

6

KARINA

"I'll go with you," Noah promised, his hand resting gently on mine. "We'll get Geneva's sapphire ring. *Together.*"

Tears filled my eyes at his generosity. Noah owed me nothing, and yet he was offering to help me with no strings attached. Words couldn't say how grateful I was. Especially since I'd never imagined when I'd woken up this morning that so much would change so quickly.

After Annika had killed Laila, chaos had erupted in the throne room. I'd used the moment to slip out of there and run to the wolves' hidden camp—the camp that I knew the location of because I'd been secretly working with the wolves the entire time I'd been in the Vale.

My king—King Nicolae of the Carpathian Kingdom

—had sent me to the Vale the moment he'd received the letter requesting he send two princesses to compete for Prince Jacen's hand in marriage. But he hadn't sent me to become the prince's bride.

No—the king had other motives. He wanted me to work with the wolves in their quest to bring down the Vale. He believed that once the Vale was brought down, Queen Laila would have no choice but to come crawling to him, desperate and homeless and looking for someone to take her in.

Nicolae had been obsessed with the queen since before I was born.

In return for my help, he'd promised that he would allow me to make a wish on Geneva's sapphire ring—an object he was confident Laila possessed.

But he'd been wrong. *Annika* possessed the sapphire ring—not Laila.

The moment the Nephilim had driven the stake through the queen's heart and Laila had dissolved into ashes, I knew deep in my soul that Nicolae would never forgive me for the queen dying on my watch.

The Carpathian Kingdom was my home, but I would never be welcomed there again.

So I'd run straight to Noah—the wolf shifter who was known in camp as the First Prophet. The moment he saw me run into camp, he'd been quick to let me into his tent.

"Why are you helping me with this?" I asked him. "You have no reason to want me to bring Peter back."

Peter was my soul mate. We'd fallen in love over a century ago, and with his permission, I'd turned him into a vampire so we could have an eternity together.

A few years later, he was killed in the Great War.

His loss had shattered my heart. I could never be whole in a world where Peter didn't exist.

But he might not be gone forever. Because Geneva was the most powerful witch in the world—she was so powerful that she'd scared other witches to the point that that they'd banded together to lock her inside the sapphire ring. She was the only one who might have magic strong enough to raise the dead.

Whoever owned the ring had command over Geneva.

Which meant if I wanted Peter back, I needed to get control of that ring.

"I might not have a reason to want Peter back." Noah was so earnest when he looked at me—this man would truly do anything for me, even if I didn't ask him to. "But I have many reasons to want you to be happy. If that means helping you get this ring so you can bring back Peter, then that's what I'll do."

"Are you sure?" Guilt wracked my soul, because I recognized the way Noah was looking at me—he was looking at me like a man in love.

I trusted him, yes. And there was no denying that I was attracted to him. I would have to be blind not to appreciate his rugged good looks.

But I could never love him, since my heart would always belong to someone else.

"I'm sure," he told me, his eyes firm with resolve. "And we shouldn't wait. So let's get Marigold in here so she can get us to the Haven."

7

KARINA

"Absolutely not," Marigold said after we'd told her our request. She was a young witch, and frail as well, so her firm resolve had caught me off-guard.

"Why?" I asked. "Geneva's ring won't just help me—it'll help *all* of us."

"Transporting both of you halfway around the world will use up a significant amount of my magic," she explained. "And unless you've forgotten, I'm the *only* witch at camp helping the wolves. My magic is keeping us hidden from the vampires so they can't use their witches to track us and kill us in our sleep. If I use up my magic by taking you both to the Haven, I won't be able to protect the camp until I've recharged. It'll leave us too vulnerable. I'm sorry, but I *must* stay here."

"Fine," I said, since her answer made sense, and the last thing I wanted was to leave the wolves vulnerable to an attack. "Then I suppose we'll have to travel the human way."

"Maybe not," Noah said. "I have a witch contact at the Haven. Perhaps she can take us."

"Which witch?" I asked, since during my many years, I'd naturally come into contact with a few residents of the Haven.

"Shivani," he answered. "I got in contact with her after the last time we spoke—when you advised me to reach out to Prince Jacen to discuss the possibility of his convincing the vampires to leave the Vale. I was going to tell you the next time we saw each other, but then you came running into camp this morning…" He shrugged, and I easily picked up the pieces of what he was going to say next—me catching him up on what had happened in the Vale had taken priority.

Marigold crossed her arms and narrowed her eyes. "You didn't move forward to talking with the prince, did you?" she asked Noah.

"I did." He stared at her, not budging despite the irritation in Marigold's eyes. "Is that a problem?"

"Of *course* it's a problem." She huffed. "The vampires of the Vale cannot be reasoned with. You and the others know what our Savior has said—the vampires of the Vale *must* be cleared from the land in order for Him to rise."

"I know this as well as anyone." Noah didn't break his gaze from hers. "I was the first one to receive a dream from Him, as you and everyone else knows. But if there was a way to work this out with the vampires without killing them—if I could convince them to leave the Vale voluntarily—then I had to try."

Relief flooded through my veins at the possibility of Noah having spoken with Jacen, since the last thing I wanted to do was have been a part of killing members of my own species.

I'd hated what I was doing from the beginning.

But I'd done it, because I would do *anything* for the chance of getting Peter back.

"You spoke with the prince?" I asked Noah, so excited at the possibility that I jumped straight ahead. "How did it go?"

"I did." He nodded. "The prince listened to everything I said, and seemed to understand. He said that he'll try his hardest to convince the vampires to leave. But he isn't the ruler of the Vale—Laila is. Well, Laila *was.* Now that Laila's gone, I assume much has changed."

"*Everything* has changed." I ran my hands through my

hair and paced around the tent, frustrated at how out of control this situation had become.

A part of me wanted to return to the Vale and help Jacen convince the vampires to leave. The more lives I could help save, the better.

But Annika had Geneva's ring, and she'd taken the ring to the Haven. Who knew how long she would be there? The faster I could get to her, the better.

Until I had the ring—and until Peter was back—everything else would need to wait.

I stopped pacing and faced Noah. "Shivani won't take us to the Haven," I said, returning back to the original point of this conversation.

"Why not?" Noah asked. "She brought both me and Jacen there so we could have our discussion."

"She brought both of you there for the purpose of establishing diplomacy within the supernatural world," I said. "That's why the Haven exists. By bringing you both there, she was doing her job. The reason I want the ring is personal—it has nothing to do with diplomacy. The witches of the Haven will know that, and they won't help me. Which means I need to get there myself."

"The human way," Noah repeated what I'd said earlier, watching me steadily. "Which means what, exactly?"

Looking at him now, I remembered what Noah had told me when he'd first taken me to see the camp—about how the wolves of the Vale were only now getting in touch with their human sides. For all of his life—and for the lives of the pack members—they'd lost touch of their humanity and had been purely wolves. The dreams sent to them by their Savior had given them faith and a common goal—the hope of Him rising had sparked their connection with their humanity once more.

Noah had never been outside of the wolves' land in the Vale. Which meant I doubted he'd ever been in a car, let alone an airplane.

"By plane," I said it simply, not wanting to insult him in case I was wrong. "I normally charter private planes, but if King Nicolae knew I was flying from the Vale to the Haven, he would know something was amiss. We'll have to fly commercial. It'll be uncomfortable, but it'll get us where we need to go."

Of course, that was assuming that King Nicolae hadn't gotten word of Queen Laila's death yet and hadn't frozen my bank account. All of my money came from the Carpathian Kingdom. Once cut off, I would have nothing.

I shivered, not willing to think about the possibility yet.

There was only one thing I could allow myself to think about right now—getting that sapphire ring.

"Very well." Noah nodded—if my inclination was correct that he'd never been in a plane before, he certainly was being calm about it. "We'll leave now."

"You'll do no such thing," Marigold said, and both of us jerked our heads around to glare at her.

"I'm the leader of this rebellion—not you." They were the harshest words I'd ever heard Noah speak to the witch, and he even let out a low growl as he took my hand in his. "Karina has been instrumental in getting us to where we are now. The two of us are leaving, and we're leaving *now*."

"You cannot." Marigold blocked the exit, standing her ground. "Like you said, you're the leader of this rebellion. The wolves look to you for support and guidance. They need you here at camp—not traipsing around the world with a vampire princess who's blinded by love for her dead husband who's never coming back."

I flinched at her words, which felt like a knife to the heart.

Peter *would* come back. I was going to make sure of it.

"You can't leave your people." Marigold focused on Noah, ignoring me completely. "You know as well as I that while they're putting on a brave face for this war, many are scared. Especially the children and the weaker fighters. You give them hope of better times to come. What message will it send if you leave them to help Karina? A *vampire*?"

I clenched my fists at the degrading way she spoke of me, my nails digging into my palms. Before being sent here to help the wolves, Marigold had been a witch of the Carpathian Kingdom. I'd barely spoken to her during her time there, but I'd seen her around enough to know that she'd been quiet and submissive.

Now she spoke of my entire species like she thought we were trash.

"*Princess* Karina." I leveled my gaze with hers, hoping to remind her of her place. "You will address me as my station demands."

She narrowed her eyes at me, but then her expression softened, and she bowed her head. "Your Highness," she said, her voice weaker than before. "I meant no disrespect. However, I feel strongly about what I'm saying. Noah is the face of this rebellion. Do as you must by going to the Haven, but his people need him here. I know it, and I believe you both know it as well."

I glanced at Noah. The fierceness in his gaze when he looked at me was all I needed to see to know that he would do whatever I asked. And the truth was, his people *did* need him here. His company would be welcomed on my journey, but I didn't need him with me. I could do what I needed to do on my own.

"Marigold's right," I said, and the witch smiled smugly. "I'll go on my own. You need to stay here. Your people are counting on you to lead them."

"Are you sure?" He pulled me closer to him, his eyes begging for my honesty.

"I am." I nodded, not wanting him to doubt my words.

He stared at me for a few moments, studying me. "All right," he finally said. "I'll stay here. As long as you promise me one thing."

"What's that?" I asked.

"That once you get that ring—once you get your wish and Peter has returned—you'll let me know you're okay."

"I can do that," I said, since of everything he could have asked, it wasn't much at all.

My heart panged as I looked around the tent, realizing that this might be the last time I was here. I believed the wolves would win the upcoming war—the vampires' numbers were smaller and they were vastly unprepared—but one never knew how a war might turn. And who knew if I would get back before the final battle?

"Be safe," I added, and then I headed out the door, not wanting him to see the tear that fell down my cheek at the realization that we might never see each other again.

8

ANNIKA

Mary's cabin was a small and efficient studio—a living room, a tiny kitchen, and an alcove with a bed. The light hardwood floors added brightness, and her furniture was neutral, simple, and functional.

The space was the right size for a college student on a budget—not for the leader of a kingdom.

"Our cabins aren't designed for guests," she said, apparently noticing my surprise as I looked around. "We have common areas decorated to impress visitors. I normally would have taken you there, but given the... abnormality of the current situation, I thought it best to come here."

Of course, by *abnormality*, she meant me. More specifically, me being a Nephilim.

I stood there awkwardly, unsure where to go. Her

cabin was pristine and clean, making me suddenly aware of the blood-splattered mess I was after fighting and killing those vampires in the Vale.

I couldn't wait to shower and wash their deaths off my skin.

"Please, have a seat." Mary gestured to her sofa, which was so simple and functional that it looked like it could have come from IKEA. "Can I get you some water?"

"That would be great," I said, realizing for the first time how thirsty I was. I hadn't had anything to drink since downing the combination of vampire blood and transformation potion that morning.

I couldn't believe that only a few hours had passed since then. It felt like a lifetime ago.

"Nothing for me," Geneva said.

In the time I'd been with Geneva, I'd never seen her eat or drink. I supposed a side effect of having a spell put on you that forced you to remain inside a ring for decades on end was that she no longer required food or liquid to survive.

Mary went to the kitchen to get my water—it was an open floor plan, so the kitchen was basically in the living room—and I sat down on the sofa. I placed my stake on my lap, unsure what to do with it. I felt safe with Mary, but I kept a hand on the weapon at all times, a gut instinct telling me I could never be too careful.

Especially when I was surrounded by supernaturals.

Even Geneva's presence was making me twitchy, and I *knew* I could trust her.

The witch sat on the opposite side of the sofa, perched on the edge and refusing to look at me. I couldn't imagine what I could have possibly done to her to make her act like this. Was there some reason why she didn't want to be at the Haven?

I'd have to ask later, when Mary wasn't around to listen to our conversation.

Mary returned with a full glass and pitcher. I downed the glass in a few gulps, glad she'd had the forethought to bring the pitcher. I was quick to pour myself a second glass, but I had only a few sips before placing it down on the table in front of me.

"I apologize again for the vampires' reaction when you appeared in the courtyard," Mary said, situating herself in the chair closer to me. "As I'm sure you know, when vampires come to live in the Haven, they agree to forgo human blood for animal blood. Many actually come to the Haven because they can't get ahold of their bloodlust and they need to live in a place where they won't be tempted to kill."

"So there's never been a human in the Haven?" I suddenly felt like an idiot for coming here.

"We have spells around the property to keep humans from wandering onto our land," she said. "We're a safe haven for supernaturals—not for humans, and certainly not for Nephilim. But luckily for you, I've been expecting you."

"How?" I asked. "And how am I a Nephilim? Until this morning, I was human. Or at least I *thought* I was human."

I clutched the stake, this all still not seeming real. I'd been a human my entire life. But I couldn't deny the surge of power I'd felt after killing Laila—and the natural instinct I'd had to fight those guards. I'd always been a strong athlete, but I'd never been able to do *that*.

Something had changed in me. I needed to know more about what that change was, and *why* it had happened to me.

"I promise I'll tell you soon," she said. "First, I want to learn more about you, and what brought you here today."

I nodded, although I looked around the cabin, suddenly feeling trapped. I'd come here because whenever anyone ever spoke of the Haven, they spoke of a kingdom that represented peace and trust. But Mary had said it herself—that peace was for supernaturals only.

Supernaturals *hated* the Nephilim. Why would the supernaturals of the Haven be any different?

I'd transported myself straight into the den of another enemy.

No *wonder* Geneva was so pissed off at me.

"Is there something wrong?" Mary tilted her head, seeming truly concerned.

She didn't *look* like someone who wanted to kill me. Then again, looks could be deceiving.

But if she wanted me dead, why had she stepped in when her vampires were trying to attack me? I wanted to believe that meant she wanted to help me, but after all my time spent in the Vale, I knew better. She was more likely trying to gain my trust so she could turn on me later. After all, I was in control of the one object that all supernaturals apparently wanted more than anything else in the world.

Geneva's sapphire ring.

I was so eager to have someone to trust that I'd followed Mary straight into her cabin. Luckily this didn't seem to be a trap, but for all I knew, it could have been.

If I wanted to survive—which was starting to look

like would be unlikely—I needed to play by the supernaturals' rules.

"I want to trust you." I spoke strongly and confidently, not allowing my gaze to waver from hers. "But I can't do that without a blood oath."

"I expected as much." She gave me a small, approving smile. "I can promise that while you're on the grounds of the Haven, I'll do everything I can to protect you. I will not harm you, and I won't conspire with anyone with the intent to harm you. I'm on your side, Annika. You have an important role to play in the future of the world, and I *want* you to succeed."

"What kind of role?" I swallowed down fear—the way she said it made it sound daunting.

"I'll tell you soon," she said. "First, I need you to trust me. Do you agree to the terms of the blood oath?"

"I do," I said.

She dashed to the kitchen and returned with a knife—she used her vampire speed, so it took only seconds. She sliced the palm of her hand, and then handed the knife to me.

"Quickly," she said. "Before our cuts heal."

From the way she said it, I assumed accelerating healing was another benefit of being a Nephilim.

I did as she said, making an identical cut in my own palm. It stung, but I breathed through the pain, not wanting to show any weakness. I held my palm up, not wanting the blood to drip on any of her furniture.

"I swear that while you, Annika the Nephilim, are on the grounds of the Haven, I'll do everything I can to protect you, I won't harm you, and I won't conspire with anyone with the intent to harm you," Mary said, her eyes locked on mine. "Do you agree to this blood oath?"

"I do," I said, and then she gripped her hand in mine.

A warm light rushed through my body, binding the promise.

When she pulled her hand away, both of our cuts were healed.

9

ANNIKA

Now that Mary had sworn her allegiance, I caught her up on everything she needed to know—starting from my kidnapping, and ending at Laila's death.

"I killed the three guards, and then reached for the ring and commanded Geneva to bring me here," I concluded. "That's how I ended up in the courtyard."

"Very interesting." Mary eyed me up, as if seeing me for the first time. "A unique story indeed. But there's one part that piques my curiosity the most."

"Which part is that?" I asked.

"To keep up your disguise while you were in the palace, you needed to drink vampire princess blood and transformation potion each day," she said. "From what I know about witchcraft—and I know quite a bit, since I've been around for a few centuries—the vampire blood and human DNA needed to have been fresh each day. How was that managed?"

"I don't know." I turned to Geneva, since she was the one who had that answer—not me.

The witch still had her back to me, refusing to meet my eyes.

"Geneva?" I said her name softly, not wanting to startle her.

"Yes, *master*?" She hissed the last word, leaning back on the sofa and crossing her legs away from me.

She'd always had her fair bit of sass, but this was a whole new level, even for her. However, I needed answers. And at this point, I wasn't above using my command over her to get them.

"Answer Mary's question," I said. "I command you."

"I kidnapped a vampire princess and two random humans," she said simply. "I brought them to an abandoned supernatural prison—one that used to be used by Nephilim—and kept them there to get their blood and DNA each day."

"What?" I gasped. "You never told me any of this."

"You never asked." She stared right at me with a look that could kill.

"Which vampire princess did you capture?" Mary asked.

Geneva leaned back and crossed her arms, saying nothing.

"You'll need to ask her," Mary told me. "She's not bound to answer to me."

"Answer Mary's question," I told Geneva. "You'll answer *each* one of our questions until this conversation is done."

"Princess Stephenie." She looked at Mary as she spoke, not at me. "The princess of the Vale was partying in the Tower, so drunk on tequila that it was easy to sneak up on her and transport her to the prison. She's known for disappearing for days—sometimes weeks—at a time. No one would come looking for her. She was the perfect princess to use for the plan."

I'd never met Princess Stephenie, but I'd heard of her a few times—both when I was a blood slave in the human village and passing myself off as Princess Ana in the palace. Princess Stephenie was a young vampire— only a few decades old. She'd been turned soon after the Great War had ended. And what Geneva had said was true—Princess Stephenie spent more time traveling than at home, hopping between all the kingdoms and who knew where else.

She'd been absent during Jacen's selection process, but everyone assumed she was out on another one of her jaunts and would return home eventually. If she'd remained missing, surely it would have raised suspicion, but Geneva was right. No one had seemed overly concerned about the jet-setting princess's whereabouts.

"The princess and the humans are still alive?" I asked Geneva.

"Of course." She shrugged, still refusing to look at me. "They needed to be kept alive so I could get the ingredients for the potion."

"They need to be set free," I said. "At once."

"That might not be a good idea." Mary held up a hand, and both Geneva and I looked to her.

"Why not?" I asked.

"Those two humans now have knowledge of the supernatural world," she said. "We can't simply let them loose. Who knows what they'll do or say?"

"Good point," I said. "Then what *should* we do with them? We can't bring them here, since humans aren't allowed in the Haven."

"In normal circumstances, that's true," she said. "But these are hardly normal circumstances. We need to figure out what to do with them, and to do that we'll need them brought here. We can have Geneva cast a spell around my cabin to contain their scents, as to not alert the other vampires of their presence. Once they're here, we'll figure out how to proceed."

"Very well." I turned to Geneva, ready to give her the

command. "You're to free Princess Stephenie and drop her off at the Vale. Then you need to return to the prison and transport the two humans to this cabin, making sure to cast a boundary spell around it so the residents of the Haven won't smell the human blood. This is all to be done as quickly as possible, starting now."

"Your wish is my command," she said, her tone dripping with sarcasm.

She gave me one final glare, and then she was gone.

10

CAMELIA

I ADDED the final ingredient to the potion and stirred it until it was mixed in. Then I stepped back and glanced at my watch.

Thirty minutes. That was how long the potion needed to sit until it would be ready for me to drink.

Once I drank it, I wouldn't have to worry about any chance of becoming pregnant.

I wished I could look back at losing my virginity to the faerie prince with disgust—after all, he'd tricked me into it with the deal we'd made—but I couldn't do that. All I could remember was the softness of his lips on mine, and the way my body had welcomed his as he'd slipped himself inside of me. The pleasure I'd experienced with him in that magical faerie garden had been unlike anything I'd ever known.

It was faerie magic—it had to be.

Even so, I couldn't deny that I'd enjoyed it.

I paced around the living room, trying to push the memories of my time with Prince Devyn out of my mind. I had more important things to worry about right now.

Such as Queen Laila being dead.

With Laila gone, my chance of becoming a vampire princess was gone with her. But now that she was gone, she could no longer keep me in the Vale, forcing me to use an obscene amount of magic to uphold the boundary.

At the rate I was going, I would use up all my magic within ten years.

For all of my life, leaving had never been an option. Queen Laila would have sent the vampire guards after me to bring me back. She would likely have invoked help from the other kingdoms, too.

If I'd left, I surely would have been dead long before I'd have a chance to die from exhausting my magic.

I'd been *so* close to getting Geneva's sapphire ring. Once I had the ring, Laila would have been bound by the blood oath we'd made to turn me into a vampire princess. But no—Laila had to go and act all smug in front of the human girl. She'd wanted to demonstrate how indestructible she was, and how foolish the human had been to think she could kill an original vampire.

The last thing any of us had expected was for the human to be a Nephilim. The Nephilim were supposed to be extinct. They'd all been killed in the Great War.

But apparently, at least one of them had lived.

It explained why Annika had been able to enter the Crystal Cavern and survive. The Crystal Cavern was deadly to all supernaturals and humans on Earth… but Nephilim weren't *from* Earth. Their human part was, but Nephilim had angel blood in them—and angel blood was from Heaven.

But I couldn't just pace around thinking about the past. I needed to figure out what I was going to do with my *future*.

With Laila gone, I was free. I could go anywhere I wanted and use my magic for *me*—not because a vampire monarch was forcing my hand.

I looked around my quarters—lavishly designed, holding everything I owned in the world—and realized that I had no idea where I would go. I'd been born here, and had never lived anywhere else. My family was dead, and everyone I knew and cared about was here.

The Vale was my home.

And right now, the wolves that lived in the surrounding land were preparing to attack.

If I left the Vale now, the boundary would come down and the wolves would slaughter everyone who lived here. I couldn't do that. But I also couldn't continue using my magic as much as I'd been. If I did, it would eventually kill me.

I would have to get help from the other witches of the Vale. None of them were close to as strong as I was, but with their help, we could maintain the boundary together. That was how all the other vampire kingdoms maintained their boundaries. But Laila had always been against that—she'd thought it was safer to have one extremely well guarded witch maintaining the boundary than multiple. According to her, multiple witches made the Vale more vulnerable to attack.

But Laila wasn't here anymore—I was. And now, for the first time ever, I had a long, full life ahead of me.

All I needed was for the other witches of the Vale to help me maintain the boundary. I knew them—I was friends with them and they respected me—so I had no doubt that they would rise to the task.

I would go to them soon. First, I needed to wait for the potion to finish brewing and drink it. Because I couldn't risk getting pregnant with Prince Devyn's child.

After the deal I'd made with him, I could never get pregnant at all.

Because my first-born child was promised to the fae.

I hadn't had time to think about the repercussions of that deal yet. After all, when I'd *made* the deal, I'd assumed I was going to become a vampire princess. I'd thought that living a full life as a witch would be impossible.

With Laila dead, everything had changed.

I glanced at my watch, impatient to drink the potion and get it over with. There were still fifteen minutes to go.

Suddenly, someone knocked on my door, flinging it open without giving me a chance to say a word.

My guard Marc stood in the frame, as commanding and intense as ever. "You need to come with me now," he said before I could rip into him for bursting into my quarters without permission. "Princess Stephenie has returned."

11

JACEN

I'D JUST FOUND the concealment charms in Laila's quarters—with the help of the other vampire princes of the Vale, Scott and Alexander—when a guard came in and told us that we needed to come to the dungeons at once.

We arrived there around the same time as Camelia.

Princess Stephenie was behind the bars of a prison cell, cuffed to the wall. She looked like a disaster and smelled even worse.

"Why is my sister being kept in a prison cell?" Scott's angry voice filled the room.

Technically, the other vampire princes and princesses of the Vale were my brothers and sisters, but I never referred to them as such. After all, I barely knew them. I especially barely knew Stephenie, since she rarely spent any time in the Vale at all.

I think Stephenie and I had had two or three conversations, at the most. But when I'd seen her, she'd always been decked out like she was preparing to walk the red carpet. She was beautiful, of course. In her human life, she'd been a movie star—she'd been considered the most beautiful woman in the world.

Then Laila had turned her and staged her death. The public believed Stephenie had died in a horrible car accident in the height of her fame.

Now, my glamorous, ex-movie star "sister" wore rags that were covered in her own waste, her skin was caked with dirt, and blood was smeared on her face. Fresh blood—the scent of it was as strong as Stephenie's rotten stench.

"Princess Stephenie was found at the start of the human village, where she'd drained two humans and was starting on her third," a guard said. He wasn't someone I recognized, and he definitely wasn't one of the guards who had been present in the throne room this morning. "My partner and I were able to stop her and bring her in."

"You didn't compel the guards away?" I asked Stephenie in shock. The princess wasn't a warrior, but she knew how to use her compulsion.

"I lost control of my bloodlust." She shrugged. "I know what happens to me next. But if you'll give me the chance, I can explain. Where's Queen Laila?" She looked around, clearly expecting the queen to appear at any moment.

"The queen is away on business," Scott said smoothly.

If I didn't know any better, I would have believed him.

He and Alexander had been informed about what had happened in the throne room immediately afterward. Even though they weren't present at the time, as princes of the Vale, they needed to know.

At first they'd been shocked, but they'd agreed with the decision to keep Laila's death under wraps until we established a new chain of command.

They'd also agreed that if any of us could gain Annika's trust to get her to leave the Haven, it would be me.

Scott turned to face the guard, and continued. "Thank you for your service. My brothers, Camelia, and I will see this through from here."

The guard bowed and left us alone.

"Erect a sound barrier around us," Scott instructed Camelia once the guard was gone.

Camelia muttered a few words in Latin and gave a flick of her hand. "Done," she said.

Scott nodded at her in thanks, and turned to Stephenie. "You haven't lost control of your bloodlust since you were first turned," he said. "What happened? Where have you been?"

"I was drugged and kidnapped," she spat. "A witch brought me to a cell to rot. It was some sort of abandoned supernatural prison. She brought me a squirrel each day—she made me live off *squirrel blood*." She shuddered, as if recalling the disgusting taste. "It was just enough to keep me alive, but barely. Most of the time she kept me drugged up on wormwood. And while I was knocked out, she took my blood."

"How do you know she took your blood if you were knocked out?" I asked.

"There were two others—humans—in the cells across from me," she said. "They told me."

"Did this witch happen to have chin length dark hair, bangs, and ice blue eyes?" I asked.

Stephenie's head shot up, and she glared at me. "You know her."

"I've seen her," I said. "Once. This morning, when she transported Annika to the Haven."

"You think the witch who kidnapped Stephenie is Geneva?" Alexander asked.

"Geneva?" Stephenie gasped. "You mean the witch that Laila—"

"Yes." Scott held his hand up, stopping her from continuing. "The one and only. But more importantly, the two humans in the prison with you—what did they look like?"

"One of them was a middle aged woman—she was nothing special," Stephenie said. "The other was in her early-twenties. She was pretty, I suppose. Maybe even pretty enough to be an actress."

I tried to imagine the witch and the humans Stephenie described, realization dawning on me. "The younger human's hair," I started. "What color was it?"

"Red," Stephenie answered. "At least, that's what it was before all the dirt caked onto it."

"Princess Ana," I said, and when I looked at Scott and Alexander, they nodded in affirmation.

"What?" Stephenie looked at me, my brothers, and then back at me again. "Who's Princess Ana? And why didn't Queen Laila send anyone to rescue me?"

"You go off to places all the time, never checking in for weeks," Scott said. "We had no idea this time was anything different."

"But if no one rescued you, then how did you get here?" Alexander asked.

"The witch transported me here." Stephanie shrugged. "She popped into my cell, dropped me off in the center of the human village, and disappeared before I could go after her. That was when I was hit with the scent of all the blood…" Her eyes went dark, and I had a feeling she was remembering the moment the bloodlust had taken hold.

I'd experienced the same thing myself, back when I was first turned.

"Given your predicament, your reaction to the human blood was understandable," Scott said. "You're not going to be held responsible for their deaths."

"Isn't that Queen Laila's call to make?" Stephenie asked, glancing around. "Where is she, anyway? She needs to be informed about what happened to me."

"Much has happened in the Vale while you've been gone," Scott said. "We'll get you out of here so you can go to your quarters and clean up. Once you're ready, we'll be waiting for you in my room. There's much to discuss, and no time to lose."

12

JACEN

"You can't be serious," Stephenie said. "The queen can't be gone."

After getting Stephenie out of her cell, she'd hurried to clean up—it had taken her an hour, tops. For her, that was fast. We'd met in Scott's quarters and had told her everything that had happened in the time she'd been gone.

"We wouldn't lie about such a thing," Scott said. "Laila's gone and the Nephilim have returned. Other than the guards who were there this morning—who have been compelled to tell no one about what happened—we're the only ones who know."

"That's not true," Stephenie said. "Annika and Geneva know, too. Who knows how many others they've told in the Haven."

"You're right," I said. "We can't keep this secret for long. If the citizens of the Vale find out before we have a chance to tell them, they'll have less trust in us than they already do."

"Families are still trickling out after the wolf attack," Alexander added. "They don't feel safe here anymore. They're leaving for the Haven."

"Unless we take a stronger stance against the wolves, more will follow," Scott said. "We need to put the wolves back in their place—sooner rather than later."

"They're trained fighters, and their numbers are higher than ours," Alexander said. "Most of the vampires in the Vale don't know how to fight, and our humans are worthless in battle. If we fight the wolves, we'll lose."

"Why are the wolves suddenly rebelling?" Stephenie asked, breaking back into the conversation. "We've lived in peace for centuries. We haven't broken the treaty Laila signed with them when she first settled in the Vale —we've stayed in our designated land, and they've stayed in theirs. Their sudden hatred of us makes no sense."

I hadn't yet told any of them about my meeting with Noah. The meeting had only happened last night, and so much had happened since then.

But with Queen Laila dead, perhaps I could do what Noah suggested—perhaps I could lead the vampires and humans out of the Vale and settle on unclaimed land. It could be the start of a fresh kingdom—a kingdom that didn't turn humans against their will, and didn't strip humans of their rights. Most importantly, we would no longer be in danger of war from the wolves.

I wasn't sure if the others would go for it, but I needed to try.

"A few weeks ago, some of the wolves started receiving visions," I started, and everyone in the room looked to me, waiting for me to continue. "The visions are from someone they call their 'Savior.' Apparently, the packs have been at constant war amongst themselves forever. Their Savior has promised that once He rises, He'll bring peace and prosperity to the wolves of the Vale. But there's a catch. Before the Savior rises, He's demanded that all vampires are cleared from the Vale. That's why the wolves have decided to kill us all. They feel like they *have* to do it to give their Savior the chance to rise."

Stephenie looked at me like I was crazy. Camelia stared blankly at her glass of wine, which for some reason, she hadn't touched. Alexander's eyebrows were furrowed, and Scott watched me closely, as if waiting for more.

"How do you know this?" Scott finally asked.

"I met with their leader last night," I said. "His name

is Noah, and he was the first wolf to receive a vision. He calls himself the 'First Prophet.'"

"Seriously?" Stephenie scoffed and threw back the remainder of her wine, reaching for the bottle to pour herself a fresh glass. "He sounds like a cult leader—not a ruler."

"He was surprisingly civil—for a wolf," I said.

"Where did you meet him?" Scott asked. "Going into wolf territory is dangerous. I assume you know that."

"I didn't go to their territory," I said. "I know that would be dangerous. Noah sent a witch envoy to bring me to the Haven, where we had our meeting. He had an interesting proposition, although I told him Laila would never go for it. But now that she's gone…"

"What was the proposition?" Scott was apparently eager to get the point.

"We can leave this land and go somewhere else," I said. "Somewhere that *isn't* already inhabited. Further north, or maybe even south, to the States. We have a lot of options—all of them better than war with the wolves."

"Absolutely not." Stephenie crossed her arms, her expression sour. "The Vale is a respected kingdom, and more than that, it's our home. Look around at everything we have—the palace, the town, even the human village! We can't leave all of this behind. If we do and go somewhere else, we'll have to start from scratch. We'll have *nothing*."

"Our sister makes a good point," Scott said. "Plus, centuries ago, Laila and the wolves signed a treaty. We've done nothing to break that treaty. This land is rightfully ours. If we leave, we'll look weak. We *must* stay and fight."

"We'll die." I leveled my gaze with his, unwilling to back down. "You weren't there in the square when those wolves attacked. I was. It was chaos. So many of our people were slaughtered before the wolves were finally brought down. We've been living in peace for too long—the vampires of the Vale don't know how to fight. And the wolves only want to kill us as long as we remain on this land. If we leave, we live. Isn't that what's important?"

"We'll have run from battle and will be the laughingstock of all the kingdoms in the world," Scott said. "The wolves are animalistic and lack all control. There's a way for us to beat them. We just need to figure out what that way is."

"And until we do?" Alexander asked. "We can't hide Laila's death forever. We're going to have to tell everyone—before they hear it from somewhere else."

"We'll spin the story," Scott said. "We'll tell everyone that Laila went to the wolves to discuss peace, and that they killed her. Not only will it explain her death, but it'll make our people more fired up to defeat the wolves."

"A smart plan," Stephenie said. "But there's still a major point we haven't yet discussed."

"And what's that?" I asked.

"Now that Laila's gone, who's the leader of the Vale?"

13

CAMELIA

"I AM," I said the first words I'd spoken since this meeting began.

The four of them—Scott, Alexander, Jacen, and Stephenie—turned their heads to look at me all at once. Their eyes all showed the same emotion—shock.

"What?" Stephenie was the first to speak. "You can't rule the Vale. You're a witch."

"I was Queen Laila's closest confidante," I said, since despite the fact that Laila kept me as a willing prisoner as long as I kept up the boundary, it was true. "Not only that, but I'm the one who keeps this kingdom safe from harm. Of course I should step up as queen. It makes the most sense."

"You're mortal," Scott pointed out. "And while we're grateful for the sacrifice you make to protect this kingdom, we all know you only have a decade left, maybe a few years more on top of that if you're lucky."

"A witch can't rule the Vale," Alexander added. "This is a *vampire* kingdom. We must be ruled by a vampire."

"It has to be one of us." Scott looked around at his siblings, his gaze serious. "One of the vampires in this room."

"Not me." Stephenie tossed back another glass of wine—she must have polished off four glasses by now. "I know my strengths, and ruling an entire kingdom isn't one of them. I'll leave it up to the three of you to decide."

"I'm also going to step out of the running," Jacen said, which surprised me—out of the three brothers, I thought he would make the most fair ruler. "I've only been a vampire for slightly over a year. The two of you have far more experience than I do. It should be one of you."

Scott nodded, apparently pleased with Jacen's answer.

But there was one big factor he apparently hadn't considered.

"A prince can't rule the Vale." I sat straighter and matched their fierce gazes with one of my own, refusing to be dismissed by the vampires again. "All of the other kingdoms are ruled by an original vampire—even the Haven. Only an original can turn humans into vampire princes or princesses. A prince or princess can only turn humans into regular vampires who can't use compulsion. Without being ruled by an original vampire, and therefore not being able to create any more princes or princesses, we'll be the weakest kingdom in the world. We'll lose all the respect and rapport we have with the other kingdoms."

"There are only five original vampires remaining, and they each already have a kingdom of their own," Scott said. "An original ruling the Vale isn't an option. It *must* be one of us."

"You're wrong," I said, smiling smugly. "An original vampire ruling the Vale *is* an option."

"How so?" Stephenie raised an eyebrow, clearly doubtful.

"I'm a powerful witch," I said. "I'm certainly strong enough to perform the spell on myself that will turn me into an original vampire."

"I thought the knowledge of that spell was lost?" Scott asked. "That's why no more witches have been able to turn themselves into vampires."

He was right—the spell *had* been lost. When the original vampires had bargained with the fae for a spell that would make them immortal, they'd agreed to give the fae all of their memories in return for the spell. They'd cast the spell, and then their memories had been taken.

No one knew the details of the spell except for the faerie who had given it to them. And from what Prince Devyn had told me of that fae, she *loved* collecting lifetimes of memories.

There was no way in Hell that I was giving up all of my memories. Memories make us who we are. Giving them up is basically the same thing as suicide.

Which meant I needed another way to get the spell.

However, the only reason I knew all of this was because Laila had told me. And before Laila had told me, we'd made a blood oath where I'd promised that I wouldn't reveal what she'd told me to anyone.

Blood oaths lived on even after death.

If I told the others what I knew, my blood would turn against me and kill me. So I would need another way to get the spell—a way that didn't involve divulging Laila's secret.

"It's true that knowledge of the spell has been lost," I started. "But there's one person in the world who might be powerful enough to know the spell—Geneva. We just need to get control of her ring. Once we have control of it, even if she *doesn't* know the spell, we can command her to acquire it for us."

Even though I was bound not to tell anyone what Laila and the other original vampires had done, I could always pretend like going to the fae to bargain for the spell was *my* idea. Then I could command Geneva to go to the fae and bargain away all of her memories in return for the spell.

"We're getting that ring," Jacen spoke up. "I'm going to make sure of it."

"Good." I nodded. "Once you have it, you'll give it to me so I can get started."

"My brother will do no such thing." Scott's voice filled the room—he sounded like he already thought he was king. "That ring will come directly to me. Once I have it, I'll command Geneva to do as you wish. If you're able to become an original vampire, then we'll accept you as our queen."

"We will?" Stephenie pouted, clearly disagreeing with him.

"We will," he said firmly. "Camelia is correct that if the Vale isn't ruled by an original vampire, we'll be seen as a second tier kingdom in comparison to the others. We might not even be seen as a kingdom anymore at all. It's the best interest of *all* of us—and for our kingdom—for Camelia to acquire that spell and turn herself into an original vampire."

"Now that we have the concealment charms, I'll meet with the guards to solidify our plan." Jacen moved forward on his seat, clearly ready to get started.

"Not so fast." Scott held up a hand, stopping him. "Before you leave, you'll need to make a blood oath."

"What sort of blood oath?" Jacen froze, suspicion dawning in his gaze.

"An oath that once you get custody of Geneva's sapphire ring, you'll kill Annika and will immediately return to the Vale to give the ring to me."

"Deal." Jacen didn't falter.

I was impressed. Scott had clearly proposed the oath to ensure that Jacen was truly on our side. After all, it had been no secret that when Jacen had first met the irritating human, he'd had a soft spot for her.

At least he was rational enough to realize his mistake, given that Annika had played him for a fool and was actually a Nephilim—a creature whose sole purpose in life was to kill supernaturals.

"Fantastic." A small smile crept across Scott's face. "In the meantime, I'll serve as acting king of the Vale. Does anyone in this room contest my right to do so?" He looked mainly to Prince Alexander—the only one of his siblings who hadn't said he didn't want to be king.

Prince Alexander said nothing, giving his older brother only a single nod of acceptance.

"Perfect," Scott said, leaning back in his seat. "Now, someone fetch me a knife. We have a blood oath to make."

14

ANNIKA

I HAD SO many questions for Mary, mainly about how it was possible that I was a Nephilim when all of the Nephilim were supposed to be dead, and about why I'd only come into my powers this morning. But Geneva was back in minutes with both humans in tow, so I'd have to wait to ask my questions until later.

I'd known what the humans would look like—I'd been disguised as the redhead the entire time I was pretending to be Princess Ana, and Geneva had been disguised as the older woman.

The humans she brought look nothing like I'd expected. Their clothes were filthy, and their hair was tangled and stringy. They were covered in dirt, grime, and their own waste, the stink overpowering the entire cabin. The stench was so strong that I could barely breathe.

The older woman stared at us in shock.

The redhead bolted for the door. She was fast—for a human.

Mary rushed past her in a blur, blocking the way out before the human had a chance to blink.

That didn't stop the girl. She raised her arm up, getting ready to punch.

Mary's hand was wrapped around her wrist in a second. "We're here to help you," Mary said calmly. "There's no need to fight us."

As if the human ever stood a chance.

"Okay." The girl was surprisingly calm. Her back was facing me, but she sounded like she might even be smiling.

Mary let go of her grip and lowered her hand down to her side. She relaxed when the girl didn't try to run again. "I'm sure you have many questions," she said. "We'll answer them all after you freshen up. I'll show you to the washroom." She headed to a nearby door—one that I assumed led to the bathroom.

The girl followed. But once they were halfway there, she bolted for the door again.

Again, Mary blocked her path, moving in a blur.

The girl screamed and tried to hit Mary again, but her attempt was futile.

Mary held both of her wrists in a second, holding her in place. "What's your name?" she asked the girl.

The girl stood completely still, saying nothing.

"What's your name?" Mary repeated, although this time, she sounded different when she spoke. There was something fuller—more musical—to her voice.

She was using compulsion.

Normally, when vampires used compulsion, they sounded no different than normal. There was only one explanation for why I could suddenly tell that she was using compulsion—it must be one of my heightened abilities as a Nephilim.

"Raven," the girl said automatically.

"It's nice to meet you Raven," she said, still holding onto her wrists. "I'm Mary, and I'm the leader of the place where you are now—the Haven."

"What *are* you?" Raven asked.

"You're not going to panic after I answer your question," Mary said, once again infusing her voice with compulsion. "I'm a vampire."

As instructed, Raven didn't panic. The older woman crossed herself and muttered a few words in prayer.

"I assume you have many questions," Mary continued. "My friends and I will happily answer them for you.

But first, the two of you need to get cleaned up. I only have one washroom, so you'll need to take turns. I'll set some clean clothes in there as well. We'll answer your questions once you're both cleaned. Now, I'm going to let go of your hands, and I recommend that you don't try to escape again. Like I said, my friends and I want to protect you. But if you leave this cabin, the tiger shifters outside will immediately maul you to death and eat you alive. Unless, of course, the hungry vampires get to you first…"

She let go of Raven's hands, and this time, the redhead didn't fight or run.

This time, she looked properly terrified.

"Very good." Mary smiled. "Now, come. It's time for the two of you to get cleaned up."

15

ANNIKA

ONCE RAVEN and the other human—Susan—were cleaned up, they sat down with us in the living room.

They both wore the same loose fitting, all white outfit that Mary and the other vampires I'd seen in the Haven wore. Since they were in Mary's size, the pants were short on Raven and too tight on Susan, but both of them had managed to squeeze into the clothes.

A shower had done them both wonders, and they now looked just like the versions of them that I'd expected. Raven didn't try to run again—I supposed Mary's threat of tiger shifters and hungry vampires was enough to make the fiery human realize that escaping would be futile.

Once they seemed as comfortable as they were going

to get given that they were still in a room with their abductor, a vampire, and that there was no hope of escape, the three of us told them everything.

"So you truly had no idea what *she* was doing to us?" Raven asked me once we were done, glaring at Geneva.

"I didn't," I confirmed. "If I knew she was keeping you prisoner, I never would have gone through with the plan."

I briefly remembered one moment when I'd almost asked Geneva how she was getting the vampire blood and making the transformation potion for me each day, but I'd been interrupted before I'd had a chance. I don't know what answer I would have expected, but the thought had never crossed my mind that Geneva had taken them prisoner in some abandoned supernatural prison, telling them nothing of why she'd taken them and leaving them to think they were going to die there.

I'd assumed that if Geneva had to do something so inhumane and horrible to follow through with my command, she would have told me so I knew exactly what I was asking of her.

I was starting to realize why the witches had wanted to stick Geneva in that ring all those decades ago and throw the ring into a cave that no one was supposed to ever be able to access.

"I believe you," Raven declared.

"You do?" I was shocked at how easily she'd trusted me, given the circumstances. "Why?"

"I'm good at reading people." She shrugged. "Plus, your story is so far out there that I sort of *have* to believe it. If you were trying to lie to me, you would tell me something normal—something I would be more likely to buy into. It's either that, or you're all crazy. And given that I've seen some of your powers already, I know that's not the case."

"I suppose so." I smiled slightly, since she had a good point. "I truly do feel awful about what you went through. I didn't intend to hurt innocents—especially not any humans—but I'm still the one who made the wish. So it's my fault. For that, I'm so, so sorry."

Beyond telling us her name, Susan had barely said a sentence this entire time. And she'd only told us her name because Mary had compelled her to do so.

I assumed she was still in shock.

"She wasn't like this when she was first brought to the prison," Raven said, glancing at Susan. "She was confused, but she *spoke*. Then she saw the vampire—Princess Stephenie—suck all the blood out of that squirrel, and something broke in her. She hasn't been the same since."

"What she saw goes against everything she's ever

thought possible," Mary said. "It makes sense that she's in shock."

"It does." Raven nodded, her eyes strong and determined, and sat straighter. "And you say you're on our side. So—what do you plan on doing to make this up to us? Because after everything we went through, you owe us a *lot*."

"I suppose we do." I sat back, thinking about my answer and trying to put myself in their positions.

After I'd found out about supernaturals, what was the one thing I wanted most of all?

I'd wanted my regular life back. I'd wanted my family back, and to return to my regular routine of school, gymnastics, and homework. I'd wanted to go to college —University of Florida had been my top choice, but of course, I had some backups in mind as well. I'd wanted to compete in my college gymnastics team. I hadn't been sure what I'd wanted to major in yet, but my parents had told me that was okay—I could take all the general requirements to get them out of the way and hopefully figure out my major from there.

All of that had been ripped away the moment vampires had cornered me and my family on that ski vacation over a year ago, killing my parents and brother and kidnapping me to become a blood slave of the Vale.

If we hadn't been on that exact ski trail at that exact

time, my family would still be alive, and I would be starting the second semester of my freshman year of college.

Because my family had been killed, I could *never* get my life back. But Raven and Susan's families hadn't been harmed because of their kidnappings.

They *could* return to their regular lives.

They just needed to forget about everything that had happened to them since they'd been taken by Geneva.

"I have an idea," I said to Raven, who was watching me expectantly. "Would you mind if I spoke with Geneva and Mary privately first to make sure it's possible?"

"That's fine." She glanced around the tiny cabin. "Where should we go?"

"No need to go anywhere," I said, and then I turned to Geneva. "Create a sound barrier around me, you, and Mary so the humans can't hear us."

"Done." Her voice was clipped and icy.

"They can't hear us?" I needed to make sure before continuing.

"Correct."

"Good." I turned to Mary, who was much more receptive than Geneva. "I think we should wipe their memories of everything that's happened to them since being kidnapped."

"It makes sense," Mary agreed. "I can compel them to forget everything since then. But they've been gone for so long that we'd have to replace their memories with something else—a reason why they've been gone. A potion would be more effective than compulsion to replace their memories with new ones."

"I assume you can make this potion?" I asked Geneva.

"I'll need the right materials, and the potion will take a few hours to brew, but yes," she answered.

"We have all the materials you'll need in our apothecary," Mary told her. "I can call on one of our witches to bring you there."

"Perfect," I said, and then I turned to Geneva, needing to make it official. After the stunts she'd pulled so far, I needed to be extra careful about how I phrased my commands. "You're to go with Mary's witch to the apothecary and immediately create the potion to erase all of Raven and Susan's memories from the moment you captured them and replace the memories with stories we've approved. Once the potion is complete, you'll immediately return here and give it to us. You'll go nowhere else but the apothecary and this cabin."

"My witch will remain in the apothecary with you the entire time you're brewing the potion," Mary added. "Once the humans have taken the potion, I'll have witches of the Haven return them to their homes."

She didn't say it directly, but the implication was clear—if Geneva went off-plan, Mary would find out, and there would be consequences.

"Once they're home, you're not to get near either of the humans ever again," I told Geneva. "Understood?"

"Yes, master." Her tone was laced with sarcasm.

"Perfect." I turned back to Mary, ignoring Geneva's attitude. "I doubt they'll like what we have in plan for them, but I truly believe it'll make them happier in the end."

"As do I," Mary said. "I've been alive for centuries. In my lifetime, I've compelled away memories of the supernatural from many humans. None of them ever *want* to lose their memories, but it makes most of them happier in the end."

"Most?" I asked. "What about the others?"

"There are always a handful that spend the rest of their lives searching for something they know is there, but can't quite remember," she said. "It's occasionally gotten them into trouble. But that's the exception, not the rule. And the rule is always the safest bet when it comes to decisions like this one."

"It's probably best that they don't ask any more questions," I said. "Can you compel them to go to sleep?"

"I can," she said. "But sleep is another one of those

things that's best handled by a potion—not by compulsion. Don't worry, though. I've got it covered." She pulled out her phone, tapped on the screen a few times, and held it to her ear. "I need you to bring two doses of sleeping potion to my cabin right away," she said to whoever was on the other side of the line. "I give you permission to teleport straight inside."

A few seconds later, a woman appeared in the center of the cabin. She had dark hair and skin, and she wore the same all-white outfit as everyone else in the Haven.

"Bring down the sound barrier," Mary told me, and I repeated the command to Geneva, who did as I asked.

"Two sleeping potions." The witch held up the vials and smiled at Mary. "Just as you asked."

"Sleeping potions?" Raven's eyes went wide with alarm. "You're giving those to us?"

"Relax," Mary said to the humans, her voice full of compulsion. "Stay where you are. When I hand you your vial, you'll drink it with no complaint."

She walked over to the witch and took both of the vials. When she handed a vial to Susan, the older woman uncapped it and drank the potion just as instructed. Before she had a chance to fall, Mary caught her mid-air and laid her down on the bed. With her vampire speed, it took her only a few seconds.

Then she took the second vial and handed it to Raven.

The girl took the vial as she was compelled to do, but she was slow, as if trying to fight off each movement. "You betrayed me," she said to me, her eyes burning with rage as she uncapped the vial and drank the liquid inside.

She blinked a few times, as if trying to fight off the haze of sleep, but she succumbed to it a few seconds later.

I caught her and laid her on the bed next to Susan.

After all, Mary wasn't the only one here with super speed.

Guilt wracked through my body as I looked at their unconscious forms. Should I have given them a choice? I suspected Susan would have been willing to forget everything she'd been through, but Raven... I highly doubted the stubborn, fiery girl would have ever agreed.

"This was the best choice." Mary placed a hand on my shoulder, bringing me back into focus. "They're humans. You and I both know that humans never fare well in our world."

"We do." I nodded, since it was true. The only humans I knew of who knew about the supernatural world were blood slaves to the vampires.

I would never wish that life upon anyone.

Mary turned away from me, focusing on the witch who'd brought the sleeping potion. "Escort Geneva to the apothecary," she said, back to business now that the humans were asleep. "She has a memory potion to brew."

16

ANNIKA

"Geneva is hurting," Mary said the moment her witch and Geneva were out of the cabin.

"She's pissed at me." I crossed my arms, irritated at the witch for the attitude she'd been giving me all morning. "I have no idea what I did to her, but she's definitely pissed."

"You killed Laila," Mary said, and then she looked at me, her eyes widening. "You didn't know," she said. "Did you?"

"Know what?" I asked, since obviously I didn't.

"Let's sit down." She returned to her place on the couch, and I did the same, giving one more glance to the humans who were sound asleep on the bed. "Now," she said once we were situated. "What do you know about Geneva?"

"Not much," I said. "Just that she's from the time of the Great War and that she's the most powerful witch in the world. She helped the vampires and witches in the war against the Nephilim." I paused, the word Nephilim holding a lot more weight now that I *was* a Nephilim.

Had I always been a Nephilim? Or had something happened to me in the throne room—when I'd driven that stake through Laila's heart—that had turned me into one?

"I'll answer all of your questions about your kind soon," Mary said, apparently sensing my desire to know more. "But now that Geneva's not here, we must discuss her first."

"Okay." I nodded, resisting the urge to bombard Mary with a million questions at once. Because she was right. With Geneva occupied with making the memory potion, now was the time for me to learn all about this snarky, powerful witch that I'd literally had in the palm of my hand since touching the sapphire ring in that cave.

"What more do you know about her?" Mary prodded.

"After the Great War, the witches became scared of Geneva because of her power," I said. "They couldn't kill her, so they banded together and created the spell to lock her inside the ring. Then they tossed the ring into the Crystal Cavern, where no one was supposed to be able to get it. Until me, of course."

"Yes." Mary smiled. "Until you."

"I guess that's all I know about her," I said. "She helped me come up with the plan to get into the palace so I could try to kill Laila, but beyond that, she hasn't mentioned anything about her past."

And I hadn't asked. At the realization, I felt terrible.

I'd been so consumed with what I'd been doing that I hadn't bothered to ask Geneva anything about herself. Of course, with all the snark she'd given me since the moment she came out of that ring, I didn't get the feeling that she *wanted* to tell me anything about herself, but still. I should have tried.

"Do you know *why* the witches felt the need to lock Geneva inside the ring?" Mary asked.

"They were afraid of her power." I knew that much—it had been one of the first things Geneva had told me when she'd come out of the ring.

I'd also already *said* that, which left me wondering where Mary was going with this.

Only one thought came to mind—there was a lot more to this story than I knew.

"They weren't afraid *of* her power," Mary said. "They were afraid of what she was trying to do *with* it."

"What was she trying to do?" I asked.

"She was trying to become immortal," Mary said. "So she could be with Laila forever."

17

ANNIKA

"Geneva... and *Laila*?" I blinked, since I must have misunderstood.

Geneva had been helping me in my plan to *kill* Laila. Hadn't she?

"I see you're confused," Mary said. "To put it simply —back when they were fighting in the Great War together, Geneva and Laila fell in love."

"But I wanted to kill Laila," I said, stunned that my initial feeling after what Mary had told me had been correct. "Geneva was *helping* me kill Laila."

I said it, but at the same time, I was starting to realize that maybe everything hadn't been as clear-cut as I'd originally thought. The entire time in the palace, Geneva had reason after reason about why I needed to wait to kill Laila. She hadn't even seemed to have put much of an effort into figuring out *how* I was going to kill Laila.

I'd assumed the delay had been because killing a vampire queen was a difficult thing to plan.

It was only now starting to dawn on me that much, much more had been going on beneath the surface than had originally met the eye.

"Geneva was using me to get herself closer to Laila," I whispered. "She never intended for Laila to die."

"Correct," Mary said. "Geneva is extraordinarily dangerous. If that ring had gotten into Laila's hands..." She shook her head, apparently not wanting to voice the possibilities aloud.

"That was her goal, wasn't it?" I held the ring tightly on my finger, as if that could make it stay put. "She didn't want me to have the ring. She wanted *Laila* to have the ring."

"Maybe," Mary said. "Geneva's tricky—I can't say exactly what her goal was. But before she was cursed, she was determined to become immortal."

"Couldn't Laila have just turned her into a vampire?" I asked.

"She could have," Mary said. "But then Geneva would have lost her magic—and she'd be a lower rank than Laila. She wanted neither of those things. She wanted to be an immortal witch."

"Does that even exist?" I asked.

"Not that anyone knows of," she said. "But that didn't stop Geneva from trying to create a potion for immortality. You see, the story you heard is only partway true. The witches were intimidated by Geneva's power, yes, but that's not why they locked her in the ring and cursed her for eternity."

"What did she do?" My stomach dropped in anticipation.

"While experimenting with inventing an immortality potion, Geneva needed to test out her creations," Mary began. "So she kidnapped other witches—less powerful witches who lived in small covens within the human world—to use as test subjects. She kept them in the dungeon of the Vale's palace and made them drink her creations. It killed most of them, and those who survived were left in so much pain that they were driven crazy by it and eventually had to be put down."

"Oh my God." I sat there in shock, my insides twisting with horror at what Geneva had done. I almost didn't believe it, except that I knew what she'd done to Raven, Susan, and Princess Stephenie.

Geneva clearly had no limits to the terrible things she would do to get her way. I could see now why she and Laila had fallen for each other. And I'd *trusted* her. I'd thought she was helping me.

I felt like the biggest idiot ever.

"It was horrible," Mary agreed. "After each failed attempt, she kidnapped more witches to experiment on. But the witches refused to allow her to continue. They couldn't kill her—they couldn't even reach her. So they had to curse her from afar, which is an impossible task, even for the strongest witch."

"But they did it," I said, my fingers still tight around the ring. "How?"

They used their Final Spell to lock Geneva inside the ring."

"Final Spell?" I tilted my head, since I'd never heard the term before. "What's that?"

"A witch's magic is their lifeblood," Mary explained. "The stronger the witch, the more magic they have. Think of the magic like a well—a witch can use their magic until nearing the bottom of the well. Once they get too close to the bottom, they need to take a break to recharge so the well is full again."

"So the stronger the witch, the deeper the well," I said.

"Exactly." Mary nodded. "Witches naturally know how much magic they can use, and when to stop using it. But occasionally, they have the need for a spell so strong that it requires all their magic at once. If they choose to cast that spell, they deplete their magic entirely. Without their magic, they can no longer live. Thus, when a witch uses all of his or her magic at once like that, it's called their Final Spell."

I shivered at the thought of anyone feeling so desperate that they chose to do that to themselves.

"It took the strength of seven witches—each a leader of his or her coven—to band together and cast their Final Spells to trap Geneva inside that ring and send the ring to the Crystal Cavern." She glanced at the ring on my finger when she spoke of it, and continued. "They sacrificed themselves to make sure no other witches became one of Geneva's experiments. Since the ring was inside of the Crystal Cavern, they assumed it would remain there until the end of time."

"Except I was able to enter the Cavern," I said. "Why?"

"Because of your Nephilim blood," she said. "Thousands of years ago, the Crystal Cavern was blessed by an angel as a place for the Nephilim to safely store dangerous magical objects that couldn't be destroyed. The cave is enchanted so only those with Nephilim blood can leave the cave unscathed. Anyone else who enters will be cursed to die."

"Like Mike," I said flatly, remembering how Camelia had told me that my fellow human blood slave—and best friend when I'd lived in the Vale—had been thrown from the Crystal Cavern to his death at the bottom of the mountain.

"Someone you know who entered the cave?" Mary asked.

"Yes," I said. "Camelia—the head witch of the Vale—recruited him to enter. She said she thought he could do it because of his strength. But if what you're saying is true, then she *knew* he couldn't. She knew that no human could survive the cave."

"She likely didn't care about him surviving," she said. "Non-Nephilim *have* entered the Crystal Cavern before. Some of them—the stronger of them—have even managed to get an object out before the cave killed them. I assume Camelia thought Mike would be strong enough to do just that."

"He *did* manage to get something out," I said. "A piece of the Omniscient Crystal."

The piece that Camelia had looked into and learned that *I* was the one she should recruit to send inside the cave.

"The Vale has the Omniscient Crystal?" Mary's eyes widened in alarm.

"No," I told her. "One of the first wishes I made on the ring was for Geneva to steal the crystal from Camelia and bring it back to the cave."

"Smart," Mary said. "Get the crystal out of Camelia's hands so she couldn't know your plan."

"She found out anyway." I shrugged, still unsure about *how* Camelia had found everything out.

Now that I knew Geneva's history with Laila and the Vale, I couldn't help but think that Geneva had done something to get me found out. She must have figured out a way to turn on me. I thought I'd been careful about what I was wishing for, but apparently I hadn't been careful enough.

"A lie as huge as the one you were telling was sure to be found out eventually," Mary said. "If you weren't Nephilim, you would be dead right now."

I nodded, since I knew she was right. But none of this felt real. I'd gone from human to Nephilim overnight, and I had no idea how.

If anyone had the answer, an original vampire who'd been alive for centuries seemed like a solid bet.

"The Nephilim were all killed in the Great War," I said, finally getting into the *real* meat of what I'd been wondering all day. "So how am I here now?"

18

ANNIKA

"Earlier, you wondered if you became Nephilim the moment you killed Laila," Mary said. "That's somewhat true, and somewhat not."

"What on Earth does that mean?" I tried to keep the irritation from my tone, but failed. Too many questions and not enough answers were driving me insane as it was. I couldn't deal with cryptic statements from an original vampire on top of it all.

"When Nephilim are born, their powers are dormant," she said. "Their powers only ignite after their first supernatural kill."

I sucked in a long breath, the explanation making so much sense. I flashed back to the moment I'd driven that stake through Laila's heart—the way my senses had suddenly sharpened, and the way I'd taken down all of those guards at once.

"I've never fought before," I said slowly. "But after I staked Laila, it felt so natural."

"Angel instinct," Mary said. "All Nephilim have it. You'll need to listen to your instinct if you want to survive."

I looked down at the stake, which I'd been holding this entire time. After using it to stake Laila and kill those guards, I'd thought the *stake* was lucky. But that wasn't true.

Fighting was in my blood.

"It all makes sense," I said, since it did. "But there's one big thing that *doesn't* make sense."

"What's that?" Mary asked.

"The Nephilim were all killed decades ago," I started. "They're extinct. So how am I here?"

"The *active* Nephilim were killed," she said. "So were all of their children who hadn't yet made a supernatural kill. But we can only sense the Nephilim if their powers are ignited. I can only assume that someone whose powers weren't ignited slipped through our sight—likely a child so young that they had no memory of what they were—and integrated with the human world. It would explain how you're here today."

"Children?" I shuddered, barely having processed anything she'd said after that part. "You killed *children?*"

"I killed no one." Her features hardened. "None of the vampires of the Haven participated in the violence of the Great War."

"But you sat by as supernaturals killed children."

"We had to," she said. "They weren't just any children. They were children who would eventually become Nephilim."

"That doesn't mean they would have become killers," I said. "They didn't even have a chance. You all—the supernaturals—didn't give them one."

"I don't think you're fully understanding." Her voice was calm and measured, as if speaking to a child. "The Nephilim were originally created to fight demons. In the beginning—far before I or the other originals were born—that's what they did. They killed them all, ridding the world of demons forever. But once the demons were gone, the Nephilim still remained—and they needed a new enemy.

"Once myself and the other originals became vampires, the Nephilim found that enemy in us. They've been on a mission to destroy our kind ever since. It was only after seeing Geneva's strong powers that they decided that witches were too dangerous, too. So the witches and vampires came together and did what was necessary for our survival—we ended the Nephilim. Those children would have grown up to ignite their powers and kill supernaturals, *especially* after we'd been forced to fight and kill their families. The only way to prevent that from happening was to kill them first."

"So you hate Nephilim," I said, since that much was clear.

"We hated what the Nephilim had become," she said. "You can't understand because you weren't there, but the Society of Nephilim saw the world in black and white. Good and evil. They saw themselves and humans as good, and all other supernaturals as evil. Nothing could convince them otherwise, and they conditioned their children to hate supernaturals from infancy, so their prejudice could continue from generation to generation. There was no overcoming such an intense level of brainwashing. It reached a point where it was us or them. Like I said, in a situation like that, we did what was necessary to survive."

"So why are you letting me live?" I held tighter onto the stake, just in case she *did* try to attack. "Why not kill me on sight?"

If it hadn't been for the blood oath she'd made with me to promise me safety, I would have thought I was as good as dead where I was sitting.

"You haven't been brainwashed by the Society," she

said. "That's what they called themselves back in the day—the Society."

"They can't have turned everyone bad," I said. "There had to be some good ones in the Society—some who saw that a person's race doesn't make them good or evil."

At the same time, I had yet to meet a supernatural who had proven themselves completely trustworthy. The only one who I somewhat trusted was Jacen, but that was so complicated that I couldn't even fully think about it right now. And Mary *seemed* trustworthy—especially since she'd started a kingdom that thrived on peace and prohibited violence of any kind—but who knew?

The only person I could truly trust right now was myself.

"Very rarely, a Nephilim would defect from the Society," she said. "Those who did were seen as traitors. They were hunted down by their own kind and killed."

I shuddered at the realization that I was descended from such a harsh, cruel race. Angels were supposed to be kind and loving, but the way Mary described Nephilim made them sound evil.

"You don't like what you're hearing?" she asked.

"No," I said. "What you're explaining to me—I'm nothing like that."

Or was I? Hadn't I hated all the vampires while I'd been a blood slave in the Vale? Hadn't I thought that as a human, I would always be hunted by supernaturals unless I became one myself so I could have the strength to fight and kill them?

I wasn't sure what scared me more—the fact that my ancestors were so cruel, or the chance that I might end up just like them.

"I know you're not like that," Mary said simply.

Her assurance allowed me to breathe again—but it didn't placate me completely. "How?" I asked. "You just met me today. You don't know anything about me."

"I might not know you, but I've known you would arrive here for a long time," she said, and then she stood up, looking at me to do the same. "Coming here is, and always has been, your destiny. You're more important to the fate of the world than you could ever imagine."

"What do you mean?" I stood up as well, still holding tightly to my stake.

Despite Mary's promise of safety, I was in enemy territory. I needed to be prepared for whatever might come my way.

"That isn't my part to tell." She headed to the door, her back to me, only turning to face me once her hand was on the doorknob. "Come with me. There's someone I need you to meet."

19

JACEN

I PACED IN MY QUARTERS, thinking about the blood oath I'd made with Scott.

Once I get custody of Geneva's sapphire ring, I'm to kill Annika and immediately return to the Vale to give the ring to Scott.

Making the promise ensured that my vampire brothers and sisters trusted me. The magic of the oath made it so that if I didn't follow through, my blood would turn on me and poison me to death.

But I didn't intend on it getting to that point. Because blood oaths were precise to their wording, and this oath depended on one main factor—that I got custody of Geneva's sapphire ring.

The solution was simple—I wouldn't touch that ring. If I never got custody of the ring, then I wouldn't be bound to follow through with the rest of the oath. Annika would live, and I'd never have to set foot in the Vale again.

If only it could be that easy. It *would* be that easy, if it weren't for the wolves declaring war against the Vale.

I couldn't abandon the vampires and humans who would be slaughtered in that war. I couldn't live with myself if I didn't try to save them.

Luckily, Noah had promised that he'd give me a heads up before the wolves launched their attack on the Vale. Which gave me exactly what I needed right now—time. Time to go to the Haven, find Annika, and convince her to use her command over Geneva to save the innocent citizens of the Vale—both the vampires *and* the blood slaves.

After that... well, I wasn't sure *what* would happen after that. The royal vampires of the Vale would never forgive Annika for killing Queen Laila, even if Annika used the ring to save the Vale. They would hunt her forever.

But I was getting ahead of myself. There was no saying what Annika would do, since I still wasn't sure exactly where she stood in everything. Right now, I had to focus on the task at hand. I could figure out how to keep Annika alive—*if* I still wanted to keep her alive—after this war was over.

And so, I picked up my phone and called Shivani.

The witch picked up after the first ring, and we exchanged the typical pleasantries.

"I need to come to the Haven," I told her, unable to skirt around my purpose for calling her any longer. "Can you bring me there now?"

"Transporting halfway around the world and back requires a significant amount of energy," she said. "Before I come to you, I must know—why do you want to come to the Haven?"

"Someone named Annika may have recently arrived to the Haven." I didn't want to give too much away in case Annika hadn't made her arrival to the Haven public. "Do you know if she's there, and if she is, is she safe?"

"An interesting question," Shivani said. "But one I must answer with one of my own."

"Go ahead." I continued my pacing, growing more and more impatient with each passing second.

"If Annika is here, do you intend to hurt her?"

"No," I spoke without a second's thought. "I just need to talk to her. No violence—I swear it."

The line clicked off, and Shivani appeared in my quarters a second later. She wore the same thing she'd had on when I'd met her—loose fitting white pants with a matching tunic. She seemed relaxed and calm, as if casually popping by after a yoga session.

"I didn't expect to see you again so soon," she said with a warm smile.

"Thank you for coming," I said. "I take it that your arrival means you're willing to transport me to the Haven?"

"I am," she said. "Although I cannot promise that Annika will agree to speak with you."

"Just bring me there and tell her I'm there," I said. "That's all I ask."

"Very well," she said. "I believe you meant it when you said you meant her no harm. But I must warn you that if you were lying and you *do* attempt any violence toward Annika—or to anyone in the Haven, for that matter—you'll no longer qualify for our protection, and you'll be at the mercy of the tiger shifters."

"I understand."

I held out my hand to Shivani, and she transported me to the Haven.

20

ANNIKA

THANKS to the protective bubble I'd commanded Geneva to place around me upon my arrival to the Haven, none of the vampires or shifters that we passed on our way to wherever we were going tried to attack me again. Most people looked at me curiously from their windows, but then they got on their way.

Still, I held my stake to my side, ready to defend myself if necessary.

Mary eventually stopped at a cabin as far away from the others as possible. The same size as all the others, it sat at the border of the Haven, looking out to the mountainous jungle beyond. Whoever lived here had clearly lucked out with his or her view.

The door to the cabin opened before we could make our way onto the porch.

A beautiful girl who looked no older than sixteen stood in the arch. Her blood had a metallic smell that I was coming to associate with vampires—it was very distinct from the flowery scent of the witches or the woodsy one of the shifters. She wore the white uniform of the Haven, and her full, wavy hair blew around her as if she were some kind of goddess.

But she didn't look at us. She stared straight ahead, as if we were invisible.

Her eyes had a milky haze over them—she must be blind.

"Annika," she said my name, still staring blankly ahead. "I've been expecting you."

I swallowed, unsure how to respond. Mary hadn't let this girl know we were on our way, yet she'd opened the door before we had a chance to knock. *And* she knew my name.

Despite the humidity of the jungle, I couldn't help shivering at the strangeness of it all. However, an undeniable feeling—perhaps that "angel instinct" Mary had mentioned earlier—told me I wasn't in danger.

"Are either of you planning on telling me what's going on here?" I asked, looking back and forth between Mary and the blind girl. "Or are you going to leave me in the dark for the hell of it?"

"This is Rosella," Mary said, tilting her head toward

the blind girl. "She's a psychic vampire, and nineteen years ago, she prophesied your arrival to the Haven."

"What?" I said, so dumbfounded that I couldn't think to craft a better response.

"Come in." Rosella opened the door further and stepped aside for us to enter. "I can tell we have much to discuss."

Rosella's cabin was decorated in the same stark style as Mary's. But unlike Mary's cabin, which had a handful of paintings on the walls, Rosella's walls were empty.

My stomach growled at the delicious smell coming from the kitchen—pizza. Her table was set for three, as if she knew we'd arrive at that exact moment.

If what Mary had said was true and Rosella was psychic, I supposed she also knew I'd be hungry. I'd been snatched by the vampire guards on my way to breakfast, so I hadn't had anything to eat since last night. Everything had been so crazy since then that I hadn't even thought about food, but now that my favorite food was in front of me, the hunger pains hit so strongly that I wrapped my arms around my stomach to stop it from growling again.

"Please sit down." Rosella walked over to the table

and placed slices of pizza on all three plates. "And don't worry—there's a second pizza in the oven. I've heard that Nephilim have quite the voracious appetite."

21

ANNIKA

I COULD NEVER SAY no to pizza, even if I *wasn't* hungry. So as starving as I was, the offer was impossible to resist. There was even soda for me and blood for the vampires.

As I wolfed down my food, Rosella told me about her past.

She'd been born to nomadic Romani parents in the early fourteen hundreds who practiced fortune telling and palm reading. They'd been good to her—fostering her natural psychic gifts—but had died from the plague when Rosella was a teen. Rosella came down with the plague soon after her parents. She got worse and worse, the disease eventually progressing and taking her sight. Afraid she would contaminate them all, her people abandoned her on the side of the road, leaving her for dead.

"Little did they know that I'd had my eye on Rosella for years." Mary glanced at Rosella with a motherly smile. "You see, the majority of humans who claim to be psychic are merely good at reading others. They use common tricks of the trade, like making vague statements that can apply to anyone, and looking for minor clues that reveal important information about the person they're speaking with. But not Rosella. I listened as she did readings for others, always surprised by how spot on she was—down to the most specific, smallest details. She was the real deal."

As she told me the story, I recalled a conversation I'd had with one of the other vampire princesses who'd come to the palace for Jacen's selection—Isabella. Isabella had also been a psychic, with the gift of empathy. When she'd been turned into a vampire, her psychic gifts had strengthened.

"You were following Rosella because you wanted to turn her into a vampire," I guessed. "To strengthen her psychic gift."

"I started the Haven to take vampires in and offer them safety—not to turn them, and certainly not to turn them against their will," Mary said. "The only exception is for psychics, as they have gifts that can help further our cause of peace. Once Rosella was fully-grown, I'd intended on giving her a choice. But when her people abandoned her, she was so close to death that not even vampire blood could heal her. Turning her should have killed her—she was too weak to realistically survive the change—but she was so near death that I tried anyway."

"As you can see, I survived," Rosella said with a smile. "My sight, on the other hand, wasn't as lucky."

"Would you have chosen to become a vampire?" I asked her. "If you were given the choice?"

"I was never meant to have a choice," she said calmly. "Being turned into a vampire and coming to the Haven was always my destiny."

I was about to argue that we *always* had a choice, but I stopped myself. It seemed pointless to argue with a psychic.

Instead, I finished off my final piece of pizza. Mary had already finished, and had moved onto starting to clean up the dirty dishes. Rosella was right that we'd needed two pies—I'd eaten an entire one myself. I also felt strangely comfortable with Rosella. Perhaps she was right, and us meeting here today truly *was* fate.

"Now that we've shared a meal, are you comfortable speaking alone?" Rosella asked once I was done.

Unlike Mary, Rosella hadn't made a blood oath that she wouldn't attack me, and Nephilim weren't protected in the Haven. But I trusted her.

It must have been that angel instinct Mary had mentioned earlier.

"I am," I said.

"Good." Mary smiled and cleared my plate, cleaning it before I had a chance to tell her that I could do it myself. "I'll be waiting outside to escort you back to my cabin once you're done."

She finished washing my plate, and then she made her way out the door, leaving me and Rosella alone.

An awkward silence descended upon the cabin the moment Mary left. I just stared at Rosella—I didn't feel bad about staring, since it wasn't like she could see me to know I was doing it—unsure what to say. She looked so young that it was hard to believe she was hundreds of years old.

"So." I poured myself another glass of soda to give myself something to do with my hands. "I guess you wanted to talk to me so you could read my fortune?"

"I already know your fate." Rosella got up and made her way to the living room, and I followed her, since staying at the table would be rude. "I've known your fate since the moment you were born." She turned to face me, her milky eyes staring eerily ahead. "The great destiny of the Nephilim who would kill the Queen."

"Oh." I took a sip of my soda, hoping it would calm my nerves. Because truthfully, whatever "great" destiny was in store for me—I didn't want it. The only thing I *wanted* was my normal life back. I wanted to fill the gaping hole that had made a home in my chest since my parents and brother had been murdered in front of my eyes.

But I would never have what I wanted, because getting them back was impossible.

"I won't tell you your fate against your will." Rosella took a seat on the couch, never stumbling in the slightest. "You can choose if you want to learn your destiny or not. If you leave right now, I won't force the knowledge upon you. But if you sit down and join me, I'll tell you everything. It's up to you. So show me, young Nephilim —what path do you choose?"

22

ANNIKA

I GLANCED AT THE DOOR, contemplating Rosella's question.

What if I *could* go back to the way things used to be? I couldn't have my family back, of course. But Geneva was a strong witch, and despite how much she hated me after I'd killed Laila, I still had command of the sapphire ring. I could command her to create memory potions for everyone who'd been in the throne room that morning and make them forget everything. No one would know I was a Nephilim—no one would even know I was *alive*.

I could move someplace new and start over.

I imagined myself living in a small European town—maybe one in Italy or Greece—and getting a job at a restaurant. I'd take some online classes on the side to get my college degree. Perhaps I would even fall in love.

Life would be easy and simple. It would be *normal.*

But I would never be happy. There would always be that question lingering in the back of my mind—what if I'd stayed and listened to Rosella? What if I'd followed my so-called destiny and truly *did* end up doing something great—something that helped people all over the world?

Although, from what Mary had told me about Nephilim, when they'd roamed the Earth they'd done more harm than good.

"Before I choose, I have a question," I said.

Rosella raised an eyebrow, but she didn't seem surprised. "Go ahead," she said with a small tilt of her head.

"From what Mary told me of the Nephilim, they sounded terrible," I started. "They sounded *evil.* Are all Nephilim like that? Will I be like that, too?"

"No." She smiled, as if my question amused her. "You can have a great destiny, but the future isn't set in stone. You decide if you want to follow that destiny or if you want to walk away. Likewise, you choose the person you turn out to be. Good, or evil… it's up to you."

I nodded, taking in her words. Her answer was exactly what I'd needed to hear. Because ever since being taken as a blood slave in the Vale, I'd wanted to be able to defend myself. Since coming into my powers as a Nephilim, my angel instinct gave me that ability. Now, I wanted to do more.

I wanted to help the humans—like myself—who'd had their lives ripped away from them by the supernaturals. At the same time, I understood that not all supernaturals were bad, just as not all humans were good.

I refused to follow my ancestors' paths of killing supernaturals simply because they belonged to a different race.

I wanted to create change. I wanted a world where supernaturals and humans lived in harmony. A world where supernaturals were forbidden to take advantage of humans' natural weaknesses, but were always innocent until proven guilty.

Maybe it was an impossible dream, but I refused to turn down the chance to try.

"Okay." I sat down on the sofa and looked straight at Rosella, confident in my choice. "I'm ready for you to tell me everything."

23

ANNIKA

"As I've already told you, a great destiny awaits you," Rosella began. "You have an important journey to go on, and the existence of the world as we know it depends on your success. You see, a threat will soon be released, and *you're* the key to defeating this threat. Without you, all other attempts to thwart this threat will fail. No matter what, we'll end up with a different world—a *dark* world. But your decisions will determine how dark it'll get."

I sat there, stunned, absorbing what she'd said. It was so *cryptic*. I waited for her to tell me more—there had to be more—but she was silent.

"What kind of threat will I be facing?" I asked, since if I was going to be fighting something, I needed to know *what* I would be fighting.

"You'll find out in time," she said. "All you need to

know right now is that to complete your journey, you'll need to obtain the Holy Grail."

"What?" I blinked, unsure if I'd heard her correctly. "Did you just say the *Holy Grail?*"

"I did," she answered. "More Nephilim will be needed to defeat the darkness that's rising. The Holy Grail is the key to creating more Nephilim. So, in order to defeat the threat, you need the Grail."

I paused for a few seconds, taking this all in. She was seriously sending me on a quest to find the Holy Grail? I hadn't thought life could get any crazier after learning about the existence of supernaturals… but apparently I'd been wrong.

"Where exactly do I *find* the Grail?" I finally asked.

"The Tree of Life," she answered, as if it were common knowledge. "The Grail has been kept in the Tree of Life for over two millennia, where it's been protected as it waits for you."

A huge weight fell upon my chest at her words. This Tree had been protecting the Grail for two millennia because it was waiting for *me*?

This was insane.

But why would Rosella lie? I wanted to trust her—my angel instinct told me to trust her—but trusting supernaturals had gotten me into this mess in the first place.

Then I realized what I was doing—I was lumping all supernaturals together as if they were all bad. That was precisely what I *didn't* want to do. If I wanted to create peace between the humans and the supernaturals, I had to accept that they weren't all against me. After all, *Jacen* hadn't been against me. He'd told me so himself.

If I'd trusted Jacen, I wouldn't have had to lie to him about my identity in the first place. Maybe if I'd had my angel instinct back then, I would have made different choices. *Better* choices.

Now, my instinct was telling me to trust Rosella.

So that was exactly what I was going to do.

"Is there anything else you can tell me to help me get started?" I asked, desperate for another clue. If I was going to succeed, I had a feeling I'd need it.

"This quest will determine if you're worthy to receive the Grail," she told me. "You can choose one other to accompany you on the journey—*only* one, and no more—and you must choose wisely. The wrong choice means failure in your quest. The right one means you'll get the Grail and will be on track to fulfilling your destiny."

I nodded and glanced down at the sapphire ring on my hand. Geneva was the obvious choice, right? Sure, she hated me, but she was bound to obey my commands.

If I was smart about what I commanded her to do, my potential could be limitless.

Except Geneva was conniving, and I had no doubt that I was the last person in the world she wanted to serve. One wrong word that allowed her even an inch of wiggle room, and she'd figure out a way to turn against me.

It couldn't be Geneva. But Rosella had been specific—I could choose only one person to accompany me on my mission.

If I chose someone else, I would need to leave Geneva behind.

Which meant I would have to trust someone else with the sapphire ring.

Suddenly, the whites around Rosella's eyes began to swirl. She sat straighter, her mouth forming into a surprised O.

"Pen and paper," she told me. "In the kitchen. Bring them to me—now."

I scrambled to the kitchen, my instinct pulling me toward the drawer closest to the refrigerator. I opened it, and sure enough, it was the "universal junk drawer." Apparently even psychic vampires had one of those. There was a notepad and pen amidst the mess inside, and I grabbed them, hurrying them back over to Rosella.

Once she had the pen and paper, she immediately

started writing—a string of numbers, with two letters thrown into the mix. After writing the second letter—an E—she placed the pen down and pushed the paper toward me.

"What's this?" I studied the numbers and letters, clueless about what they could mean.

"That's all you need to know to get started on your quest," she said. "Your destiny awaits. And remember what I said—the world is counting on you to succeed."

As if I could forget.

24

CAMELIA

I RETURNED TO MY QUARTERS, pleased with how the meeting had gone with the royal vampires. As long as Jacen did what he'd promised—which he *would* do, since he'd made a blood oath with Scott—we would have control of Geneva's sapphire ring.

With that ring, I could command Geneva to bargain away her memories to the fae in return for providing me the spell that I could use to turn myself into an original vampire.

The plan was truly perfect. Because once Geneva had no more memories, she'd be a fresh mound of clay, free for us to mold however we saw fit.

I'd be an original vampire, I'd have control of Geneva's sapphire ring, and I'd rule the Vale.

It was everything I'd ever wanted.

Except for one small matter.

I wrapped my arms around my stomach and walked over to my bar. On top of it sat the potion that I'd created before being called away—the one that would destroy any potential baby that might be growing inside of me.

I couldn't turn into a vampire with a baby growing inside of me. It had been tried before, and it was physically impossible. A human needed to be strong to survive the change, and a pregnant body was weakened by the stress of taking care of not just itself, but the life growing inside its womb.

Every single pregnant woman who'd started the process of changing into a vampire had died before the change could complete. It didn't matter how far along they were in the pregnancy—anywhere from days to months. They *always* died.

I wouldn't survive the change if I were pregnant. And who knew if the royal vampires of the Vale would be patient enough to wait nine months for me to deliver the baby? With war looming on the horizon, they'd never wait. I couldn't know *what* they would do instead, but a pregnancy would put a huge wedge in my plans.

I reached for the vial, ready to down the potion. But I stopped before the glass touched my lips.

Could I truly make such a rash decision? I had no

more blood family left. My mother had died when I'd been a young teen from using up all of her magic, and I'd never known my father. He'd been brought to the Vale to impregnate my mother and sent back to his coven once his job was complete.

According to Laila, he'd been paid quite handsomely.

As for siblings, I had none. The more powerful a witch, the harder it was for her to get pregnant. It was the same for men—the ones with the strongest magic were the least fertile.

That's why powerful witches like myself were so rare.

That was also why I'd paused before drinking the potion.

Because if I *were* pregnant—and while it was a rare chance, there was still a chance—it might be the only chance I would ever get to have a child of my own. Especially if I became a vampire—then I'd certainly never have a child.

I didn't think I could live with the knowledge that I may have destroyed the one chance I had of becoming a mother.

Of course, there was the problem that I'd promised Prince Devyn that he could have the child once he or she came of age, but I had time to deal with that—likely years. Surely a solution could be found that would allow me to keep my child. The fae loved to bargain—there had to be something Prince Devyn wanted more than a half-blood child.

But I was getting ahead of myself. As it was, I didn't even *know* if I was pregnant yet. How long did it take before it was possible to find out?

I placed the vial down and looked it up on my phone.

The answer popped up quickly. Two weeks after conception—*that* was when I'd be able to tell if I was pregnant.

I could wait two weeks before drinking the potion.

I capped it and placed it inside my refrigerator, where it would stay fresh for at least a month. I took one last look at it before closing the door.

This was for the best. This way, I could make an informed decision. The most likely situation would be that I wasn't actually pregnant at all—besides the fact that my strong magic made pregnancy difficult, I'd only even had sex one time. I was probably beating myself up over a decision that I didn't even need to make.

I'd wait two weeks.

Then I'd find out that I'm not pregnant, and I'd no longer be burdened with such a hefty choice to make.

25

ANNIKA

I EXITED the cabin and found Mary speaking with a woman who exuded the floral smell of a witch. Dressed in the white outfit of the Haven, she had dark hair and dark skin, and she was short, her head barely coming up to Mary's shoulders.

"Hello," the woman said, giving me a small bow of respect. "You must be Annika."

"I am," I answered. "Who are you?"

"Shivani," she said. "I'm one of the witches of the Haven."

I already knew she was a witch, of course—I could smell it—but I nodded anyway to be polite. Hopefully she didn't want to chat with me as well. The paper Rosella had given me with the numbers and letters was burning a hole in my pocket. I was eager to ask Mary if she had any idea what the clue might mean, but wanted to wait until we were alone.

"I brought someone here who wants to speak with you," Shivani continued. "He's waiting in the meeting room."

"Who?" My eyes narrowed, suspicion rising in my chest. It had been hours since I'd killed Queen Laila, and everyone who'd been in the throne room had heard me command Geneva to bring me to the Haven.

By now, I expected that every vampire of the Vale was looking to kill me. Maybe vampires from other kingdoms, too.

"Prince Jacen," she said, and my suspicion disappeared, replaced with something else—anxiety.

I'd lied to Jacen so much. Surely he wouldn't be able to forgive me? I'm not sure I would be able to, if I were in his position.

"You don't have to speak with the prince if you don't want to," Shivani continued. "But remember that everyone within the Haven—including visitors—is forbidden from causing any violence while here. As long as our rules are followed, no harm comes to anyone on our lands."

It only took one glance at the tiger sauntering in the distance to remind myself about what happened to those who *didn't* follow the rules of the Haven.

"Okay." I took a deep breath, although I didn't think anything could prepare me for this. Because despite doubting that Jacen still cared for me after all my lies, I couldn't walk away.

I needed to know if there was a way I could fix the mess between us.

"Take me to see the prince."

I followed Mary and Shivani out of the residential area and back to the main square. It was daytime, and while the canopy of trees provided shade from the sun, the only people still out were the occasional witches or shifters. The vampires were probably in their cabins, sleeping.

They led me into the main building. Unlike the simple cabins I'd seen so far, the common areas of the Haven were beautifully decorated with bright, uplifting colors and fabrics. Even the floors and walls were bursting with multitudes of colors. I felt like I'd entered the set of an elaborate Bollywood film.

"At the Haven, we believe wealth and beauty should be shared—not privately owned," Mary explained as we walked. "While not working or sleeping, our citizens spend the majority of their time in the common areas."

"It's beautiful," I said.

"You should see it during the night hours when everyone's awake," Shivani said. "There's always much to do and learn, as we believe in constant growth of the spirit and mind. Our citizens fill the palace with their peaceful spirits and positive energy."

I nodded and smiled, although my stomach flipped with the knowledge that each step we took was one step closer to Jacen.

We turned down a few halls, getting further and further away from the main area. Finally, Shivani stopped in front of an elaborate door surrounded by twisting columns.

"We're here," she told me, and then she reached for the door, pulling it open.

26

ANNIKA

THE MEETING ROOM looked like an Indian tearoom designed for a maharaja and his courtesans. Jacen waited inside, and he stood when we entered.

"Annika," he said, taking a sharp breath inward when his eyes met mine.

He was wearing the same jeans and black shirt that he'd been wearing that morning. But unlike this morning, he wasn't watching me with disdain.

He was looking at me like he'd waited for years to see me again.

My heart fluttered at the possibility that all wasn't lost between us.

"Jacen." My cheeks heated as I said his name. The moment felt so personal, and I shifted in place, highly aware of Mary and Shivani standing there watching.

Were they going to stay here the entire time?

"We'll leave you to it," Shivani said, nodding at each of us. "Remember—while we won't be in the room with you, and we won't be able to hear you, there are cameras watching you. One wrong move and I'll transport here with the tigers before either of you can blink."

"Understood." Jacen's eyes remained locked on mine, and the hairs rose on my arms at the intensity of his gaze. "Although I assure you that there's nothing to worry about."

"It's always better to be safe than sorry," Mary said, and then she and Shivani exited the room.

The door closed, and Jacen and I were left alone.

My instinct pulled me toward him, urging me to do only one thing—*trust* him.

But I stood there, unmoving, unsure where to begin. Because this was the first time I'd spoken to him as me— as *Annika*—since we'd fought the wolves together outside the Vale. So much had changed since then. I was a completely different person than I was then—a completely different *species*.

"I'm so sorry," I blurted out, desperate for him to believe me. "I should have trusted you from the beginning, when you risked everything to help me escape. I wish I had. Everything would have been so different if I had. I'm so, so sorry that I didn't."

"Why didn't you?" he asked, his expression hard and unreadable. "Since finding out you were alive, I've been thinking about it constantly, and I just don't get it. So please, Annika. Help me understand what happened."

He was willing to listen. Good. At least that was a start.

"Can we sit?" I asked, since telling him everything meant we would be here for a while.

"Of course." He sat on the nearest bench—it was covered in colorful pillows that hardly matched the mood of this dark conversation. He sat straight and alert, clearly on guard around me.

His distrust in me hurt, but at the same time, I couldn't blame him.

I situated myself in the bench across from him. Between us was a coffee table with a pitcher and some snacks on it. Neither of us moved for the food or drink. I laid my stake down next to me—it was the only thing I had to protect myself, and even though I trusted Jacen, I didn't intend on letting the weapon leave my side.

"You lied to me," he started. "I thought I was bad for pretending to be human when I was a vampire. I felt like I'd taken advantage of you—the poor, innocent human who'd been left weak and alone and was just trying to have a fun night out with her friends. Meanwhile, you were getting the last laugh, since you weren't exactly human, either. Was this all some giant plan of yours? I mean, since you're a Nephilim, you must have known I was a vampire the moment we met. Right?"

"I didn't know," I told him. "I didn't find out I was Nephilim until this morning. Before then, I was a human. At least, I *felt* like a human. My powers were only activated once I killed Laila."

He tilted his head, as if out of everything he'd expected me to say, it certainly hadn't been *that*. "How am I supposed to believe you?" he asked. "You've already lied to me about so much."

"I'll tell you everything from the beginning," I said. "If you're willing to listen."

He crossed his arms and watched me expectantly, as if daring me to continue.

I swallowed, preparing myself to begin. This was it—Jacen's trust hinged on me telling him every last bit of the truth.

I refused to mess this up.

"Everything I told you when I was Annika was true," I told him. "But after we were caught trying to leave the Vale, everything changed. Because the vampires didn't kill me. They brought me to the dungeons, and Camelia came to me with a deal—if I went to the Crystal Cavern and got her Geneva's sapphire ring, she'd have me turned me into a vampire. She even made a blood oath on it. I couldn't say no—since being kidnapped to the Vale, all I wanted was a way to protect myself so I wouldn't be a victim to the supernaturals ever again. You knew that—I'd *told* you that—but you'd refused to turn me. Camelia was giving me that chance. I didn't know if I'd ever get the opportunity again, so I took it."

"But you never gave her the ring." He glanced at the object in question, which was currently displayed on my finger. It was bright and gaudy—so unlike anything I would ever buy for myself. "You kept it for yourself. Why?"

"When I was inside the Crystal Cavern, it caved in." I shrugged, as if it had been no big deal.

In reality, it had been terrifying.

Concern flashed across his features, but he regained control of himself a moment later, the emotion replaced with guarded coldness. "It caved in randomly?" he asked. "Or did you do something to make it cave in? So Camelia would think you were dead and you could keep the ring for yourself?"

"I didn't do it on purpose." I couldn't help but feel shocked at his accusation. But then again, after all my lies, I supposed it wasn't fair to blame him for assuming everything I'd done had been part of a giant scheme. "Although, maybe I caused it unknowingly…"

I hadn't thought about it much before—I'd had so much else to worry about. But now that Jacen asked, certain things started to click into place and I realized that yes, I *might* have done something to trigger the cave in.

"There were bats in the cave." I shivered at the memory of them flying down from the ceiling and coming for me. "They started attacking me. I wasn't supposed to touch anything but the ring—Camelia had warned me as much before I'd entered the cave—but I wasn't about to let myself be bitten to death by bats, either. So I reached for the nearest weapon—a sword—and used it to attack them back. After I struck the first one, they flew back up to where they'd come from, and the cavern caved in."

"You were lucky to survive." Pain flared in his silver eyes when he looked at me—as if the thought of my death hurt him. But I had to be imagining it. Because he hated me for lying to him.

Right?

Of course, the flicker of emotion was gone before I could analyze it further.

"The cave in blocked the only exit," I explained. "The main area with the artifacts was okay. It must have been some kind of spell put on the cave by whoever created it."

Which would be the angels, if the story Mary had told me was true.

"You used the ring to escape," he assumed.

I nodded and pulled the ring closer to my side, since he was right.

"You should have had Geneva take you as far away from the Vale as possible and never looked back," he said. "That was your chance to find safety and leave everything in the Vale behind. But you didn't. Why?"

"Because my family is gone." I swallowed away the lump that formed in my throat every time I thought about them. "I had nothing left to go back to. Even if I did, how could I possibly return to a normal life after everything I'd been through? I couldn't. But with Geneva's ring, I could help so many people. I had to try."

"You could have died trying," he said, a shadow flashing over his eyes. "You still might, now that people know you're a Nephilim. You're going to be hunted forever."

Darkness descended upon my mind, because he was right. Being a Nephilim gave me strength, but what good was that strength when so many supernaturals surely wanted me dead?

I shook the thought away. Worrying about it now would only lead me to spiral deeper and deeper into the hopelessness of it all. I had to focus on my goal—getting Jacen to believe the truth.

"I'd already been hunted—when the vampires took me to the Vale," I said. "You don't know what life is like as a blood slave there. I do. The fact that I'd been chosen by Camelia to get the ring was pure luck. I couldn't let the ring go to waste. I had to do what I could do to help the other blood slaves—to try to free them. I wouldn't have been able to live with myself if I'd just saved myself and left them there."

"So why didn't you come straight to me?" he asked. "I'd risked my *life* trying to get you out of the Vale, and you knew I'd been turned against my will. I would have helped you. I thought I'd done enough to prove that."

"I *was* going to come to you," I said. "But then Geneva looked into the Omniscient Crystal. She showed me how Camelia had used transformation potion on Tanya to make her look like me, and had her killed to fake my death. And then she showed me how you reacted to my death…"

Understanding flashed over his eyes, and from there, I told him everything about my time as Princess Ana, up to the moment I'd come to the Haven.

27

ANNIKA

"We've been on the same side the entire time," Jacen said once I'd gotten him up to speed. "We were just being too dense to realize it."

"Good thing I ended up being Nephilim." I gave him a small smile, but it hardly did anything to lighten the mood. "Otherwise, I'd be dead right now, and you never would have known the truth."

"I wasn't going to let you die in that throne room," he said. "You know that, right?"

He watched me so closely that I felt dizzy from the intensity.

How had I ever believed that Jacen didn't care about me?

"I'd *hoped* so," I said, winding my fingers around each other as I spoke. "But you didn't exactly jump up to my rescue in there, either."

"You proved you didn't need rescue." He glanced at the stake next to me. "And I knew that as long as they didn't have the ring, they wouldn't kill you. They wouldn't risk killing Geneva. But if they'd gotten that ring…" He clenched his fists, and his expression hardened, as if imagining what he would have done. "I would have done *anything* to keep you safe."

"Even though I lied to you?" I asked.

"I knew there had to be some kind of explanation," he said. "And I was right."

"You were." I smiled for real this time, feeling at ease around him for the first time since I'd come in here. "Thank you for hearing me out."

"I didn't have an option," he said. "Curiosity gets the worst of me sometimes, and when it came to you, I *needed* to know the truth. But there's still one thing you haven't told me."

"Oh?" I raised an eyebrow. "What's that?"

"You never told me about how you came to work with the wolves."

"What?" I asked. "I wasn't working with the wolves."

"Someone in the palace was," he said. "It was the only way the wolves could have gotten through the boundary to stage that attack."

"If someone was working with them, it wasn't me," I

said. "The only times I'd ever seen the wolves was when we fought them in the forest and when they attacked the town. Both of those times, they were trying to kill me. I swear I wasn't working with them. I'll even make a blood oath if that's what it takes for you to believe me."

"I believe you." He held a hand up in a stop motion, and my heart warmed at his trust—it was something I'd wanted for longer than I'd realized. "But if you weren't working with the wolves, then why did that one stop before attacking you?" he asked. "And don't pretend you don't know what I'm talking about—I know you do. The wolf was about to attack you in the courtyard, and then it stopped. Why?"

"Your guess is as good as mine." I shrugged. "When it happened, I thought it smelled that I was a human. You know wolves can do that—they smelled past my vampire disguise when we were in the forest, too. And none of the humans in the square were attacked. The wolves only went for the vampires."

"Except that you're *not* human," he said. "You're Nephilim."

"Remember—at the time of the attack, I was human," I said. "My Nephilim blood only activated once I killed Laila."

From there, I told him everything I'd learned since coming to the Haven—from the details of being

Nephilim, all the way up to Rosella telling me about my destiny.

"It all makes sense," he said. "Except for one thing."

"What?" I asked.

"When we were in the attic of the Tavern, you resisted my compulsion."

"You tried to compel me?" I sat back, surprised—and a little annoyed that he'd tried to mess with my mind like that.

"Yes." He nodded. "When I told you to forget we'd ever met."

"Wow," I said, the annoyance only growing. "So you were going to *compel* me to forget your existence?"

"For your own good," he said. "Or at least, I thought so at the time."

"Still." I huffed and crossed my arms. "I deserved a choice in the matter."

"And I deserved to know your true identity while you were in the palace," he said. "So let's call this even, all right?"

"Fine." I sat back in agreement. It wasn't like I had to worry about him trying to compel me again, since compulsion didn't work on Nephilim. And he was right—I'd lied to him enough times that I could call this even.

"I assumed you were wearing wormwood—it was the only way you could have resisted my compulsion," he said. "But you swore you weren't. And at that time, your Nephilim powers weren't activated. So why didn't it affect you?"

"I don't know anything more than I told you right now," I said. "I promise. But maybe Mary has the answer."

"Maybe," he said. "But first, you mentioned a paper Rosella gave you with numbers. It sounded important. Can I see it?"

I pulled it out of my pocket and handed it to him.

He glanced at it and smiled. "These are coordinates," he said, looking up from the paper. "Do you have a phone on you that I can use to look up their location?"

"No," I said. "The guards took it from me before bringing me to the throne room. Didn't you bring one?"

"I did," he said. "But I have pretty good reasons to suspect that it's being tracked."

"Why would it be tracked?" I asked.

"You see, to come here without the royal vampires of the Vale suspecting me, I had to make a deal with them…"

From there, he told me everything that had happened to him from the time I'd flashed out of the throne room to now, sparing no details.

"So no matter what happens, I need you to promise

that you'll *never* give me that ring," he finished, his eyes serious. "Can you do that?"

"I promise." I rested my hand on top of the ring, cursing it for bringing so many problems into my life. "But your family's expecting you to eventually return. When you don't, they'll know you're not on their side anymore. What are we supposed to do from here?"

"We're going to ask Mary to borrow her phone so we can look up those coordinates," he said. "Figuring out their exact location is imperative to your quest."

He stood up with the paper in hand, ready to leave the room.

"Wait," I said, since there was still one big thing I needed to ask him.

"What?" He tilted his head, watching me curiously.

"I'm supposed to ask one person to join me on my quest." I twisted my fingers around themselves, nervous. We still had a lot to work out between us, but I took a deep breath and focused on him, figuring it was best to get out with it. "Will you be my person?"

"Yes." He smiled, and with that one smile I knew—Jacen and I were a team. "I will."

28

ANNIKA

"Tromso, Norway," Jacen announced, looking up from Mary's phone. "Well, a bit northwest of Tromso. That's the closest city to the coordinates."

We were still in the tearoom—Mary had been happy to join us when we'd invited her back inside. She hadn't known the answer to the compulsion question—her best guess was that my dormant Nephilim blood had protected me—but she *did* let us use her phone.

"So that's the starting place for our quest," I said. "Norway."

"It appears so," Mary said. "We can't provide a witch to get you to your location, as doing so might break the peace with other kingdoms—or even with the Vale once they discover that Prince Jacen has turned on them. But that won't be a problem, since you can command Geneva to transport you."

"Actually, I can't," I said, and she tilted her head, clearly curious for me to continue. "Rosella told me that only one other can accompany me on the quest. If I bring more than one person with me, I'm doomed to fail. I'm also doomed to fail if I bring the *wrong* person. So I've asked Jacen to join me, and he's accepted."

"But the ring..." Mary's eyes darted to the sapphire ring on my finger and then back to my face, alarm shining in her eyes. "It's no secret how dangerous it could be in the wrong hands."

"I understand." I twisted the ring off my finger and held it out to her. "Which is why I've decided to give Geneva's sapphire ring to you."

Mary stared at the ring, not moving to take it. "Are you sure about this?" she asked. "Geneva's powers could benefit you greatly on your quest, if you were careful with the wording of the commands you gave her."

"I'm sure," I said, and my angel instinct glowed warmly in my chest, as if affirming my decision. "The best place for the ring is at the Haven—where its powers won't be taken advantage of—and you're the leader of the Haven. You're the only person I trust with this ring. If you don't believe me, then I hope you can at least believe my angel instinct, because it's telling me that it *has* to be you."

"Thank you." Mary took the ring from me, and just like that, the transfer was done. "And I hope you know that if you ever need a safe space with no questions asked, the Haven will welcome you for as long as you need it."

"I appreciate it." I watched her slip the ring onto her finger, realizing that now that I was a Nephilim, I no longer needed Geneva's magic to keep me safe. I was no longer a weak human.

I was able to protect myself.

I'd had a taste of strength when I'd drank Jacen's blood, and more of it while drinking Princess Stephenie's blood to disguise myself as a vampire princess, but now the strength was truly *mine*.

Having the ability to keep myself safe was an incredibly freeing feeling. But remembering what it had felt like to drink the vampire blood made me wonder something…

"Now that I'm a Nephilim, what would happen if I drank vampire blood?" I asked. "Would it make me into a super powerful Nephilim when it was in my system?"

"Supernaturals can't drink vampire blood," Jacen replied. "But does that apply to Nephilim?" He looked at Mary to answer, since she was the only one in this room who'd been alive before the Nephilim were all killed in the Great War.

"It does," she confirmed. "Vampire blood makes Nephilim sick, the same way it does for all other supernaturals. The Nephilim are not as different from us as they'd like to think." Her eyes glimmered with amusement at that last part.

"How sick?" I asked.

"Your body would reject the vampire blood," she said. "You'd throw it up until it was out of your system."

"Yuck." I shuddered, the awful memory of that time I'd gotten the stomach bug crossing through my mind. I still remembered the final meal I'd had before getting sick—fried shrimp—and couldn't stomach the idea of eating it to this day.

It was a good thing I hadn't had pizza for that meal. I couldn't imagine a world where the thought of pizza made me nauseated.

"To thank you for giving me Geneva's sapphire ring, I'll acquire the proper forged documents for you and Prince Jacen to take on your journey," she said. "Jacen doesn't really need it since he can use compulsion, but it'll come in handy for you in case the two of you get separated. I'll also call on a chartered plane to get you to the Tromso airport."

"Thank you," I told her. "We'd appreciate that a lot."

"It's the least I can do," she said. "But remember—once you leave the Haven, you're on your own."

"No, she's not." Jacen reached for my hand and gave it a small squeeze. "Because she has me."

29

CAMELIA

"We need to send vampires to scout the wolves' location," Scott said from the head of the boardroom table. "It's the only way we can be ready with a plan of attack once we have Geneva's sapphire ring."

Laila had only been gone for a day, and Scott had already called a meeting for him to lead as acting king. The public still didn't know that Laila was dead, but when we'd told the guards that the queen had gone away for a business trip and left Scott and me in charge in her absence, they'd believed us.

Of course, the bit of compulsion the vampires had used when telling them had helped. But all that mattered was that they bought the story. Because this was the business trip the queen would never return from. It was the business trip we were going to claim had resulted in an altercation with the wolves, and therefore, her death.

It was the only way to do this. If the citizens knew that she'd been murdered inside her own palace—inside her own *throne* room—they would fear their safety more than ever. Fear led to chaos, and chaos led to the crumbling of kingdoms.

A rebellion led by our own people *certainly* wasn't something we needed to deal with on top of everything else going on.

"There's no way that can be done in a stealthy manner," I pointed out. "The wolves will be able to smell the vampire scouts. We'll just lose more fighters—fighters we can't afford to lose, given the war on the horizon."

"I never said we'd send out vampire guards." Scott smirked, and a shiver raced down my spine.

"Then who do you want to send?" Stephenie chimed in. "Civilians?"

"Bingo." Scott pointed at her and grinned. "They'll wear charms to hide their scent, like the wolves did when they attacked the Vale."

"The wolves will still be able to hear them," I said. "And see them, if they accidentally get too close. Most of them will be discovered and killed. And besides the fact that we shouldn't be putting civilians in danger like that at all, we need those charms for Prince Jacen's mission. Without those charms, we lose our chance of a sneak attack on the Nephilim, which means we lose our shot at getting the ring. It's not a risk we can afford to take."

Especially not for me, since I was depending on controlling Geneva to get the spell to turn myself into a vampire queen.

"A valid point." Scott nodded. "I suppose we'll need more charms then, won't we?"

"Those charms were made with dark magic," I reminded him. "Dark magic isn't practiced in the Vale."

"I know all about dark magic," he said. "For it to work, it requires the blood of one killed by the witch's own hand. We certainly have enough humans in the dungeons ready for slaughter, so I fail to see the issue."

I took a deep breath, annoyed by his ignorance—and his selfishness. He knew the effects dark magic had on witches. But apparently, he needed a reminder. "Once a witch starts using dark magic, it weakens their ability to perform natural magic." I spoke as calmly as I could, given the awfulness of what he was requesting. "In laymen's terms—they get addicted to dark magic. Since my *natural* magic keeps the boundary up around the Vale, and we all need that magic to keep the Vale protected, I'm unable to perform dark magic. At least, not without weakening my ability to keep us all safe."

"You're not the only witch in the Vale," he said. "Surely one of the others can do this for us."

"You can't ask that of them." I curled my fists under the table, disgusted by Scott's suggestion. "Even if you do, none of them will agree to it."

"I *can* ask it of them," he said, his eyes flashing with determination. "And I will—even if it means compelling them to follow orders myself."

"You won't be able to compel them." I instinctively reached for the wormwood pendant that I always wore around my neck. "You know very well that they use wormwood to protect themselves, just as I do."

We didn't just wear the protective charms—those were mainly for show. We also ingested wormwood daily. Living in a kingdom of vampires, it was the only way to ensure we maintained autonomy over our decisions.

"Well, then," Scott said. "I've decided upon my first command as acting king."

"What's that?" I sat as straight as possible, even though the coldness in his tone chilled me to the bones.

"Signing a new law that from now forward, not only humans are forbidden to use wormwood to protect themselves—but that witches are, too."

30

ANNIKA

MARY STOOD by her promise of acquiring Jacen and I fake papers—along with a private jet to take us to Tromso, Norway. The jet was stocked with more food and drinks than we could possibly consume, including bagged human blood for Jacen.

I silently thanked Mary for thinking of everything.

Unfortunately, I couldn't enjoy the jet nearly as much as I would have in any other circumstance. I was too busy trying to analyze what Rosella had told me regarding my destiny. Jacen listened to me and tried to help, but it was no use. Besides the coordinates, we didn't have enough information to go on to come to any solid conclusions.

By the time we arrived in Tromso, we were no closer

to figuring out an answer than we were when we'd taken off.

I shivered when I got off the plane, glad that Mary had also given me winter gear for the trip. Jacen, of course, was unaffected by the cold.

A car waited for us on the tarmac—a black Jeep Wrangler, with huge extra headlights attached to the front. I supposed those were necessary in a place where the sun was barely out in the winter.

However, the sun barely being out was a good thing, since Jacen was only at full strength at night. While vampires *could* go out during the day, it weakened them more and more the longer they were out in the sun. Jacen *needed* to be at full strength for the entirety of this mission, which meant avoiding the few hours per day that the sun was out in northern Norway.

A man stood next to the car, and he introduced himself as Tom. "Here are the keys to the Jeep," he said, dangling them in front of his chest. "Who's driving?"

"Me!" I rushed for those keys faster than a feral vampire ran at a freshly wounded human.

Jacen was by my side in an instant. "You sure about that?" He raised an eyebrow and chuckled.

"I haven't driven in ages." I pouted. "Not since being taken to the Vale. And this car…" I sized it up, smiling in approval. I'd always wanted a cool car, but my parents had insisted on getting me a boring SUV. *This* was far more in tune with my tastes. "I'm a good driver. I promise."

"I believe you," he said. "But you're also from Florida. Have you ever driven in snow before?"

I looked around at the snow-covered mountains and frowned, because he made a good point. Not only had I not driven in snow, but I'd also never driven on terrain that wasn't flat.

"Fine," I muttered, since I didn't come all this way to have the quest end in a car accident. "You can drive."

I handed the keys off to Jacen, and he swung them around his fingers, looking at the Jeep in excitement.

"There's a survival kit and some cans of petrol in the back, in case of emergency," Tom said. "You can never be too prepared in these parts."

I opened the back trunk, curious to see what we had. Water, canned food, and bagged blood—apparently Mary's special requests went far. Next to the gasoline was a kit with a flashlight, matches, a flare gun, and the like. There was a first aid kit as well—not like we'd likely need it, due to our accelerated healing abilities. There was also a shovel and ice pick—things we didn't need in our cars in Florida, but were apparently standard here.

They also could make good weapons, if necessary.

With that thought, I brought them up to the front

seat, just in case. I hoped we wouldn't need them, but like Tom said, it never hurt to be prepared.

"Ready?" Jacen said, hopping into the driver's seat.

"Ready," I said.

He plugged the coordinates into his phone—a borrowed phone, of course, since he'd left his at the Haven so the vampires of the Vale couldn't track us—and we were off.

31

ANNIKA

WE WERE ONLY five minutes into the drive, and I was already glad I'd handed Jacen those keys.

The narrow, snow-covered roads wound around the mountains and fjords—it was about as opposite from Florida driving as you could get. It was so remote that there were no street lamps, and I was grateful for the heavy duty headlights attached to the Wrangler. Even *with* our enhanced supernatural sight, it would have been tough to see otherwise.

There was apparently no direct way to get to where we were going—likely because of the mountains and fjords—and we wound around the roads so much that it felt like we were going in circles. I only knew we were driving north up the coast thanks to the GPS on Jacen's phone. When we'd started the drive, there were a handful of other cars on the road, but now there was no one but us.

I gazed out the window, glad Jacen was driving so I could take in the scenery. It was truly beautiful—I felt like we were driving through another world.

"In point five miles, your destination will be on the left," the robotic voice of the GPS lady said.

I looked around in confusion. There were no hints of civilization in sight—just the mountains to our right, and the ocean to our left.

Where on Earth were these coordinates taking us?

We were nearly to the other side of a bridge when a huge animal leapt from the mountain and onto the road.

Jacen pumped on the brakes, and the Jeep skidded to a stop only a few meters away from the animal.

Now that it was right in front of us, I gazed up in shock. Because that wasn't an animal. At least, it wasn't any type of animal I'd ever seen.

It was a *troll*.

It was as tall as a house and wide enough to take up the entire two-lane road, blocking our exit from the bridge. Its skin looked like bark, and the rest of its body looked like rocks. It held onto a walking stick, and while it didn't directly say, "Thou shall not pass," that was the vibe I was getting from its stance.

It didn't move to attack—it just stood there and

watched us, as if it expected us to turn around and drive in the opposite direction. That was what any *sane* person would have done—but we needed to get to the location of those coordinates, and judging from the map, this road was the only way there.

"Is it just me, or is that a troll?" I asked, wanting to make sure I wasn't hallucinating.

"It's not just you," Jacen confirmed. "It's definitely a troll. And it apparently doesn't want us getting to where we're going."

I reached for the shovel, ready to use it if necessary—and glad I'd brought it to the front. "Drive forward," I told him. "See if it moves out of the way."

I doubted it would move—our Wrangler couldn't take on the troll, and I bet it knew that—but it seemed worth the try. Jacen apparently agreed, because the car started to move slowly forward.

The troll slammed his walking stick into the ground straight ahead of us, and Jacen braked again. The stick was only inches from the car this time.

If Jacen had gone past the edge of the bridge, the front of the Wrangler would have been scrap metal.

"That was close," I said.

"It's not attacking us," Jacen said. "It's just not letting us past the bridge."

"We need to get by," I said. "And I don't think it'll be open to reasoning with us."

"It can't hurt," he said.

I gave him the side-eye, not needing words to let him know how insane I thought that sounded.

"It seems like a better plan than fighting it," he said. "Especially since we don't have any weapons."

I reached for the ice pick and handed it to him, keeping my grip on my shovel. "Take that," I said. "Just in case."

He frowned at the ice pick. "That big guy will crush this," he said.

"Just take it."

"Fine." He held tightly onto the ice pick and got out of the car.

I did the same, gazing up at the hideous troll looming overhead. With each step we took, my instinct told me that this *wasn't* going to work. But Jacen was right—anything was better than fighting this thing.

"Hi." I smiled and lowered my shovel, forcing myself to sound breezy and confident. "We need to continue down this road, if you wouldn't mind letting us pass."

The troll leaned down and reached forward, as if to shake my hand. His skin looked even more bark-like up close—he truly *was* made up of stone and wood—and he held eye contact with me the entire time.

I stepped forward, hoping we were establishing some kind of understanding.

The moment I crossed onto land, he knocked me to the ground and plucked the shovel from my grip, tossing it into the sea.

The hit to the ground knocked the wind out of me. But I took a pained breath inward, forcing myself to stand.

As I was getting up, Jacen ran at the troll in a blur, stabbing its arm with the ice pick.

The troll grunted and slapped Jacen to the side, as if he were a bug and not a super strong vampire.

Jacen landed on the bridge and recovered quickly, standing up and brushing the snow off himself. Now that he was back on our side of the bridge, the troll had returned to ignoring him. But Jacen still had the ice pick in hand, and he narrowed his eyes at the troll, looking ready to try again.

"Stop!" I called out to him, and he did as I said, looking at me with question in his eyes. "I think I have a better idea."

I ran to the back of the car, relieved when Jacen followed. As expected, the troll remained where it stood. Throughout all of this, he'd stayed on "his" side of the bridge. Apparently, he was purely defensive—he wouldn't attack unless we did so first.

"What's your idea?" Jacen asked. "Because that thing is as strong as a mountain. I can't think of a supernatural on Earth who could get through it."

"We're not going through it." I picked up one of the jugs of gasoline and handed it to Jacen, and then lifted one for myself. Thanks to my Nephilim strength, it wasn't heavy at all. "We're going to burn it."

"Nice." Jacen uncapped his jug and headed toward the troll before I could say more.

We both hurled the gasoline at the troll, making sure to stay on the bridge as we did so. As long as we were *on* the bridge, the troll didn't attack. There must have been some kind of magical barrier where the bridge met the land. He sniffed the air a few times as the gasoline landed on him, but other than that, he stood in place, making sure the bridge wasn't passable.

"Now for the fun part," I said once both of the containers were empty.

Jacen raised an eyebrow at me and smirked. "I never would have pinned you as a pyromaniac," he said as we walked back to the car.

"A girl's gotta have her secrets." I actually *wasn't* a pyromaniac—I was just excited to see if my plan would work—but a little flirting never hurt anyone, not even when they were fighting a troll.

I fished around the survival kit, smiling when I

found the flare gun. I'd never used a flare before, but I *had* shot a gun—we had plenty of gun shooting ranges in Florida. I used the flashlight to skim over the directions—luckily, the flare didn't look too complicated to use.

"Get in the passenger seat," Jacen told me as he climbed inside the car. "How far does that thing shoot?"

"A thousand feet," I told him what I'd read on the instructions.

"Perfect." He turned the car around and drove to the other side of the bridge.

The troll watched us, but it didn't move. I had a feeling it wasn't going to move until we were off the bridge entirely.

It apparently thought it was the Bridge Master. Up until now, it probably *was*.

But up until now, it hadn't met us.

"How close to the troll are we?" I asked, since I didn't know *exactly* how far a thousand feet was.

"Close enough to hit it," he said. "And far enough away that we won't get blown up in the blast. Are you sure you don't want me to do this?"

"Have you ever shot a gun before?" I asked him.

"Why use guns when you have fangs?" He smiled and flashed his fangs, as if reminding me how dangerous he was.

A part of me urged me to go for my stake—it must

have been my angel instinct—but I resisted. My instinct might recoil at the sight of vampire fangs, but my brain —and heart—knew better.

"I'll take that as a no," I said.

I flipped my hair over my shoulder as I got out of the car, then I readied my stance and pulled the trigger.

32

ANNIKA

THE TROLL EXPLODED INTO FLAMES.

It howled and stumbled off to the side of the road, hurling itself straight into the ocean.

I jumped back into the car and fastened my seatbelt. "Go!" I screamed, although Jacen hardly needed the encouragement to put the pedal to the metal and race down the bridge. I laughed at the thrill of the speed, adrenaline rushing through my body as we peeled down the road.

We whizzed by the place where the troll had been standing, and I turned around in time to see the creature's big ugly head surface above the water.

It huffed, as if frustrated that we got away, but made no attempt to hurry out to follow us.

Relief coursed through my veins at the fact that the

troll wasn't dead. Which was silly, I knew—that troll would have killed us if we'd attempted to fight it to get past the bridge—but I didn't want to kill if I didn't have to.

Especially since the deaths of those three vampires guards still haunted my conscious. They were just doing their jobs, like the troll was doing his. They hadn't deserved to *die*.

But I faced forward, not wanting to allow myself to spiral. We had a quest to focus on. Wallowing in self-pity wasn't going to get me anywhere.

"Your destination is on the left," the GPS lady said, and Jacen slowed the car as we approached.

The only thing on the left was an abandoned house with a rickety dock going out into the ocean. The roof sagged, looking about to fall in, and the windows were cracked and dirty.

It looked like it had come straight from a horror movie. But this was clearly where we were supposed to be—it was the only building on the road for miles.

"It's deserted," Jacen said as he pulled the car to a stop in front. "And decrepit. I wouldn't trust the floor to hold us."

"We didn't come all this way not to go in," I said, already on my way out of the car. I doubted anyone was inside—Jacen was right that it looked deserted—but I carried my stake with me just in case.

"I know that," he said, fast behind me. "We just need to be careful where we step, that's all."

I nodded and headed toward the rickety building, my angel instinct warming my chest with each step I took. "There's another clue for us in there," I said, walking faster now. "I feel it."

Jacen walked beside me, and we paused on top of the faded welcome mat in front of the door.

He reached forward to open it, but stopped himself. "This is your quest," he said, dropping his arm to his side and motioning for me to take the lead. "After you."

"Thanks." I reached for the door, but not to open it. Instead, I knocked.

Jacen raised an eyebrow, clearly thinking I was nuts to have knocked on the door of an obviously abandoned building, but said nothing.

We waited for a few seconds.

Nothing happened.

A breeze passed by, and I shivered, wrapping my arms around myself and missing the heat inside the Wrangler. I tried to peek through the window, but the glass was covered in so much filth that it was nearly opaque.

Jacen glanced back and forth between the doorknob

and me. It was clear what he was thinking—he thought I should just open the door myself.

But bursting into a home seemed rude—no matter how abandoned it appeared.

So I raised my hand to knock again… at the same time as the door started to slowly creak open.

33

ANNIKA

A BEAUTIFUL WOMAN in a hand-stitched gown stood in the opening. She looked like she'd stepped out of a fairy tale. Behind her, I got a glimpse of the inside of the house—it was bright, cheery, and full of plants and flowers.

"You must be Annika," the woman said with a smile. "Please, come in."

I stepped inside the warm cabin, and the woman took my coat, hanging it on the coat rack. Even the coatrack had greenery on it—flowering vines that traveled up its spine. The entire room smelled like an overdose of floral perfume, so strong that too deep of a breath made me dizzy. The scent covered up the smell of the woman's blood—I had no idea what type of supernatural she was, if she was one at all.

"Who are you?" I gazed around the plant-filled entry room, which seemed to glow from within. Even the windows were scrubbed clean and completely intact—far different from the cracked, dirty panes I'd observed on the doorstep. "What's this place?"

"I'm Dahlia," she introduced herself. "And this is the home my sisters and I have made for ourselves while waiting for your arrival." She turned away from me and looked at Jacen suspiciously, clearly sizing him up. "Who's your friend?" she asked.

"Jacen Conrad." He gave her hand a solid shake before dropping it promptly. "Vampire prince of the Vale."

"I didn't realize we would be hosting royalty." A smile flitted across Dahlia's face, and she tilted her head toward him, batting her lashes.

"Jacen is my chosen companion for my journey." I stepped closer to him and took his hand in mine, leaving no space between us. "He's making sure I stay safe and protected."

"I see." She glanced down at our joined hands and took a small step back.

Yes, I was staking my territory. And no, I had no shame about it.

"My sisters are waiting in the living room," she said, quickly changing the subject. "Shall we join them?"

I looked around the bright, blooming room—this lady could either be as kind as she seemed, or secretly evil, like the hag from Hansel and Gretel who lured children into her home to plump them up and eat them. I didn't feel a need to be on guard, so I suspected the former. However, I glanced at Jacen, curious to get a read on his thoughts.

He just shrugged in response, as if leaving the decision to me.

Unsure what else to do, I looked inward, toward my angel instinct. Warmth spread through my chest—a feeling I was coming to associate with the confirmation that my intuition was correct.

"That would be great," I said to Dahlia with a smile. "Thank you."

She swished her skirt and led the way toward a nearby door—it was rounded and carved of wood, perfectly in place in this fairy tale dwelling. "You'll want to mind your head once inside," she warned Jacen. "You don't want to knock into the hanging gardens."

He nodded in response, although I suspected that if he knocked into a hanging garden, it would be the garden that got hurt—not his head.

We followed Dahlia into the living room. Like she'd warned, multiple boxes hung from the ceiling like chandeliers, each one overflowing with blooming plants. Just like the entryway, every flat space in this room held plants and flowers, the scent so strong that it felt like breathing in a sickly sweet poison.

Two women in similar dresses to Dahlia's sat on opposing couches sipping tea. They shared Dahlia's brown hair and light eyes, and while they didn't appear to be triplets, they all looked the same age.

They each lowered their cups of tea when we entered.

"These are my sisters," Dahlia told us. "Violet and Iris." She pointed to each of them as she said their name. "Sisters, this is Annika the Nephilim and Prince Jacen of the Vale."

"Nice to meet you," I said.

Jacen simply nodded at them—apparently my greeting was enough for both of us.

"After all these years, you've finally arrived," Iris—or maybe it was Violet—said, looking at me in awe. "Would you like to sit down and join us for tea and sandwiches?"

34

ANNIKA

THE SISTERS POURED us cups of vervain tea—they'd grown the herb themselves—and served us mini sandwiches with the crusts cut off. I was hungry—a side effect to fighting a troll in the freezing cold, I supposed—and was quick to dig in.

Jacen didn't eat or drink anything, despite accepting a cup of tea. Did he think these women were trying to drug us? My instinct told me that they weren't, which was why I felt comfortable accepting food and drink from them, but I appreciated that he was looking out for me.

"What is this place?" I asked after polishing off a sandwich. "Are you supernaturals?" I gazed around the flowering room again, the questions escaping my lips one after another. There was clearly magic at play here —I just wanted to find out what *type* of magic.

"We are mages from the realm of Mystica." Iris gave me a small smile before taking a sip of her tea.

"Come again?" I blinked, half of what she'd said not making sense.

"Mages are the mythical ancestors of witches," Jacen said slowly. "It's rumored that they live in a realm parallel to our own, and that thousands of years ago, they came to Earth and mated with humans to create the first witches. Soon afterward, they returned to their world, never to be heard from again."

"That's halfway true," Violet said. "Because we didn't come to Earth. The humans came to us. Thousands of years ago, they discovered the entrance to the Tree of Life—the Tree that acts as the bridge between realms."

"The Tree of Life." I gasped, my cup of tea clanging with the saucer. "That's what Rosella told me I needed to find."

"Be patient—we'll get to that," Violet said with a kind smile. "Are you ready to hear the remainder of the answer to your question?"

"Sorry," I said, since while I *wanted* to jump straight to the Tree, I also didn't want to anger these women. While they seemed kind, they also seemed powerful.

It was never a good idea to piss off people who held a

lot of power—at least not if you wanted them to help you.

Violet gave a small nod, and continued. "The humans were safe in Mystica, of course, but in the other realms?" she said. "Not so much. Our kind sympathized with the humans—as we do with all living creatures—and we rescued the ones we could from the other realms, bringing them back to Mystica. Once they were all safe in our realm, we gave them a potion to erase their memories from the moment they'd discovered the Tree, and we returned them to Earth. When they were safely returned, we cast spells around the Tree of Life to prevent humans from stumbling upon it again. The Tree has remained hidden to this day."

"And the witches?" I asked. "What does this have to do with them?"

"Mages love all living creatures," Dahlia said with a knowing smile. "When the humans were in our realm, we loved them as well. Many women ended up impregnated during their stay—it was this mixing of humans and mages that resulted in the creature you refer to as a 'witch.' The human women who were impregnated had their children on Earth, and the mage women found their children loving homes on Earth once they were born."

"The mages gave up their children so easily?" I asked.

"It was the kind thing to do." She smiled again, as if the solution were easy. "In our realm, the witches would have always been weak compared to the mages, but on Earth, they would be strong. Earth was the best place for them. So, we gave them the best."

"I see." There was something eerie about these women that made the hair on my arms stand on end, but I forced a smile, since they *were* being exceptionally accommodating to us.

Plus, they knew about the Tree of Life—and I needed to learn how to get there.

"We were correct—the witches have thrived on Earth for thousands of years," Iris added. "Well, until recently. But that's where you come into play, isn't it?"

"I don't know," I told them. "All I know is what the psychic Rosella told me—that I need to go to the Tree of Life to get the Holy Grail. Then she had a vision of the coordinates for this location, wrote them down, and here we are." I looked around the strange, plant-filled room, still amazed that we were inside what had appeared to be a dilapidated building when we'd pulled up.

"We've been here since your birth," Dahlia said. "Waiting for you."

"So you could bring me to the Tree of Life?"

"No, dear." Iris threw back her head and laughed. "We won't bring you to the Tree of Life."

"Oh." I deflated, since I'd been hoping they would. "But you said your kind cast the spell to hide it, so I thought you knew where it was?"

"We do," Dahlia said. "But the Holy Grail only belongs to one who has demonstrated his or her worth to have it. Therefore, we cannot go with you. This is your task, and you must complete it with the help of your chosen companion." She made a brief nod to Jacen—avoiding his gaze—and then turned back to me. "However, we *can* start you on the path to find the Tree. Would you like to receive our help?"

35

ANNIKA

"Yes," I answered, since obviously I hadn't traveled up here for nothing. "Of course I'd like to receive your help."

"We were hoping you would say that." Violet placed her tea down on her saucer and stood.

Her sisters did the same, as if they were robots programmed to move in tandem.

Creepy.

"Come," she continued. "We have a fully stocked boat waiting out back."

They led the way, and I followed warily, with Jacen by my side. How could there be a boat waiting out back? I'd seen the back when we'd pulled up—all there had been was a dilapidated dock. There certainly hadn't been a boat.

Then again, all *this* had been was a rundown, abandoned building.

The mages clearly had magic of the likes I'd never seen—not even from Geneva herself.

They led us out back, where sure enough, a gleaming fishing boat sat attached to a shiny dock.

"How did you do that?" I looked behind us, amazed to find that the house also looked shiny and new as well.

"It's a more powerful version of the boundary spells used by the witches on Earth," Violet explained. "The decrepitude is simply an illusion. You're only seeing through it because we're allowing you to do so."

"Very cool," I said, since it was.

"I'm guessing we're supposed to leave in that?" Jacen motioned toward the boat, which bobbed peacefully next to the dock.

"Of course," Violet said. "We've had the boat waiting for you for years."

Jacen turned to me. "Do you know how to drive a boat?" he asked.

"No," I answered, since while I'd gone out on boats with friends before, I'd never actually driven one. "I'm guessing that doesn't mean you do?"

"It can't be much harder than driving a car." He turned to the mages. "Right?"

Dahlia rolled her eyes and gave us a quick rundown on how to handle the boat.

"There are supplies inside," she told us once the lesson was over. "There's water, but no blood. I hope you've brought your own?" She glanced at Jacen, then at me, and I realized her implication.

She thought Jacen was planning on drinking from *me*.

"I have a bag of it in the car." He placed his hand protectively on mine. "I don't drink from the vein, and more importantly, Annika can't afford to be weakened during this journey."

"Good." She nodded. "There's a fridge inside the boat. You'll find an ample amount of weapons to choose from."

I immediately went on guard. "Why will we need weapons?" I asked.

"You didn't think getting the Holy Grail was going to be *easy*." She smirked. "Did you?"

"Of course not," I said, although when I imagined the Tree of Life, I imagined a *peaceful* place—certainly not a place where I would need to use weapons.

I realized what a stupid assumption that was. Around supernaturals, it was *always* a good idea to have weapons. And after the encounter with the troll on the bridge, it was clear that my stake—despite having been previously owned by a powerful original vampire—wasn't going to cut it.

"How do we find the Tree of Life?" Jacen asked. "Is there a map?"

"Of course not." Iris huffed. "We couldn't very well leave a map to the Tree of Life hanging around for anyone to find, now could we?"

"No," I agreed, staying serious despite the ridiculousness of her tone. "That would be extremely irresponsible."

"It would," she said. "Especially when it's so simple to tell you how to get there. You just need to take the boat directly northwest. Stay the course, and you'll eventually reach the mist. Don't let the mist frighten you—you *must* remember that it's part of the spell to deter people from finding the Tree. As long as you hold onto that knowledge, you'll pass through unharmed."

"Thanks," I told her, secretly glad that the directions to get to the Tree weren't complicated. I doubted GPS would work in the open sea, and I'd never been good with directions. "I really appreciate your help. But I can't help from wondering… *why* are you helping us? You're from another world entirely, so why do you care if we succeed on our quest?"

"A heady question," Iris said. "Especially because the answer isn't one you're yet ready to hear."

"But we can tell you this," Dahlia chimed in. "If you fail, Earth won't be the only realm in danger. You *must* succeed—not just for Earth, but for all of us."

"Wow." I let out a long breath and looked out at the sea. "I don't know if I'm ready for this."

"You are." Jacen's gaze was strong and steady—he was confident in *me*. "You're the bravest, most resilient person I've ever met. You can do this. Fate wouldn't have chosen you if you couldn't."

"Thanks." I couldn't help but blush at the compliment—as if I were still at the palace competing for his hand in marriage instead of working with him to defeat a mysterious threat that could destroy the world as we knew it.

"We have faith in you, too," Dahlia said. It was perhaps the nicest thing she'd said to me since I'd walked through her door. "You're the final Nephilim. This destiny has always been yours."

They gave us some sandwiches to go, and then Jacen and I situated ourselves in the boat, thanked the mages again for all of their help, and we were off.

36

KARINA

IT WAS impossible to sleep on the plane flight to India, and it wasn't because the jeans and tank top I'd bought at the airport were uncomfortable, or that I'd been shoved into a middle seat in coach class like I was in a heard of cattle.

It was because all I could think about was that with each passing minute, I was getting closer and closer to being reunited with Peter.

I still had access to my bank account, so it didn't seem like King Nicolae knew yet that I'd gone rogue. The vampire court of the Vale must have decided to stay silent about Laila's death. It was a smart move—one I would have suggested myself. The Vale was in a dangerous spot with the threat of the wolves looming near—the sudden death of their leader would only result in panic.

However, it wouldn't be long until the truth came out. So I'd removed a hefty sum of cash from the bank—enough to last me for a long, long time.

Not that I'd need much of it, since compulsion was a handy way to get everything I wanted *without* having to pay.

I got off the plane—along with my backpack full of cash and my treasured mini-portrait of Peter—and headed straight for the taxi line. It was long, and full of humans who were sweaty and smelly after a long travel day.

Not even the delicious scent of their blood could cover up the awful body odor.

I ignored the line and headed straight to the man up front, despite the protests of bleary-eyed travelers who'd been waiting in the line for who knows how long.

The man looked me over and said, "You need to go to the end of the line, ma'am."

"I've received special permission to skip to the front." I spoke in the native tongue—languages had always been of particular interest to me—weaving the magic of compulsion into my tone. "Call me a taxi, now. One with air conditioning."

The air conditioning wasn't for my personal comfort—vampires were tolerant of extreme temperatures—but because I had a long drive ahead and hoped that one with air conditioning would stink less than one without.

I was wrong.

After what felt like forever, the driver arrived at the address I'd given him. It was the furthest away from civilization one could get without driving straight into the national park. There was only one small country house around, and since no lights were on inside, it appeared that its inhabitants were fast asleep.

The driver turned around and told me how much I owed.

Before he finished speaking, I leaned forward, pulled his head back, and sunk my fangs into his neck. He went limp in my arms, thanks to the calming effect of my venom. It had been so long since I'd had a drink—I couldn't take one on the plane or in the airport, at least not without drawing attention to myself—and I relished in the velvet taste of his blood. It had a nice little kick to it, as if he ate spicy foods on a regular basis.

I only took what I needed, breaking away before taking more blood than he could afford to lose. I watched as the remains of the venom on his skin finished up their job, healing the twin pinpricks on his neck. It would be sore tomorrow—as if he'd slept on it funny—but other than that, he would have no idea that anything was amiss.

I didn't even need compulsion to convince him that it had never happened. Like all humans, he was dazed enough from the venom that after emerging from the haze, he would forget everything. He'd find a logical way to explain the empty space in his memory, as they all did.

I leaned back, wiping any excess blood off my lips. "You were feeling generous today and decided not to charge me," I told him, laying on the compulsion and smiling as I spoke. "Thank you for the free ride."

"My pleasure." He smiled back at me, although his eyes were hazy from the venom and compulsion. "Have a great day."

"You too." I got out of the taxi, slammed the door closed, and watched him drive away.

I felt bad for not paying, especially after drinking from him. But there was no saying how long the cash I'd removed would last me—I might need it later for something I didn't anticipate now. I needed to save every penny I could.

I wasn't yet at the Haven, of course—the Haven was far away from any roads and enchanted to keep humans away, since the vampires there couldn't risk being near humans and smelling their blood.

Therefore, I removed my flip-flops and headed there the only way I could—I ran.

37

KARINA

The vampires of the Haven were quick to bring me to their official meeting room, where a pitcher of animal blood and a tray of snacks were laid out on the table. One whiff of the animal blood made me glad I'd had that drink from the taxi driver while I still could.

It baffled me how the vampires of the Haven survived on such rancid blood. *I* certainly wasn't touching it, although I did have some of the garlic naan with some water. Indian food had always been one of my favorites—their seasoning and spices were absolutely divine.

Back when I'd been human—over a century ago as a peasant in Romania—I never could have dreamed that food could be so delicious. I'd since made it a mission to try food from every culture imaginable.

I was still enjoying the food when the door opened, and Mary stepped inside.

I dropped the piece of naan onto my plate and stood, since the leader of the Haven outranked me.

"Princess Karina." She smiled, although her eyes were full of question. "Shall we have a seat?"

I did, although I fiddled with the hem of my poorly made shirt, feeling more nervous than ever.

"To what do I owe this honor?" Mary asked, the concern in her eyes growing stronger by the second.

I'd been planning this moment since the drive to the airport in Canada. Everything I told the leaders of the Haven would be confidential, and every vampire in the world knew that Mary was trustworthy with secrets. It was why everyone trusted her—and this place—so much. She was more than just a leader. She was the mother of the Haven, and she'd *earned* that trust.

In my present situation, I needed a safe haven more than ever.

And so, I told her everything.

"Interesting," she said once I was finished, taking a sip from the glass of animal blood that she'd poured while

I'd been speaking. "I'm not sure what I'd expected, but it hadn't been that."

"I love Peter." I sat forward, swallowing after speaking his name. "I couldn't refuse the offer King Nicolae gave me—the chance to make a wish on the sapphire ring once he had it in his possession. But the entire time I was reporting to the wolves, I hated that I was betraying the vampires. I also learned that the wolves aren't at all like I used to believe. Many of them —including Noah—are kind and good. The return of their Savior gives them hope. Who am I to take that hope away? Especially now that Laila's gone. There *must* be some kind of compromise that can satisfy everyone and avoid war."

"There's certainly a lot of work to do to ensure peace, although I always believe that there's a solution to everything—the challenge is simply in finding that solution." Mary studied me with her wise eyes that felt like they could see straight into the depths of my soul, and I fidgeted in place under her gaze. "But you're not truly here to help the Haven negotiate peace," she said. "Are you?"

"No." I looked down at my hands, my cheeks flushing in shame. "I'm not."

"I suspect I know why you're here," she said, and I looked back up at her, glad to see that she appeared to understand—not to judge. "However, if you're looking for something, you need to be the one to ask. It's only once you ask that we can try to find a solution."

"I want the same thing I've wanted since the beginning of this mess," I said. "A chance to wish on Geneva's sapphire ring and ask her to bring back Peter."

"And you know that Annika came to the Haven, because you heard her command Geneva to bring her here when you were in the throne room."

"Yes." I sat forward, anxiety rushing through my veins with how close I might be to that ring. "Is she still here? If she is, I promise not to hurt her. I'd never do that—especially not on Haven grounds. All I want is a wish on that ring. *One* wish. That's all."

I sounded desperate, but I didn't care—I sounded that way because I *was*. In the Carpathian Kingdom, we were always taught to control our emotions and rein them in. But if showing my feelings was the way to get Peter back, then I'd broadcast them to the entire world.

Guilt also tugged at my middle, because I'd told Noah that I was going to try to get that ring and bring it back to the Vale to help the wolves' cause. Which I still *might* try to do.

It all depended on Mary's answer to my question.

"Annika is no longer in the Haven," Mary declared.

I deflated. It was all because Marigold had refused to

transport me straight here. I couldn't say for sure, but I had a feeling that if I hadn't had to spend all that time traveling here the human way, I would have been here before Annika had left.

"But you don't need to be so sad." Mary held up a hand, as if that could halt my devastation.

"Do you know where she went?" I needed a clue —*anything*. This was the only lead I had on the girl, and I didn't intend on wasting it.

"I do know where she went," Mary answered. "But where she went is irrelevant for what you seek. Because while she was here, she left Geneva's sapphire ring with me for safekeeping."

"She *gave* you the ring?" I blinked, not buying that it had been as simple as that. "Why?"

"She had her reasons, and they were good ones. But surely that isn't what you care about right now?"

"No." I straightened, because she was right. "Where are you keeping the ring?"

"I'm keeping it right here."

She reached for the delicate chain around her neck and pulled out a charm that had been hidden beneath her shirt—Geneva's sapphire ring.

38

KARINA

I GAPED at the gleaming sapphire, wanting to grab it and take it for myself.

But I couldn't do that—not to an original vampire, and especially not on Haven territory—so I took a deep breath, controlling myself.

Mary wouldn't have told me she had the ring just to dangle it in my face and torture me. Of all the original vampires, Mary was by far the kindest.

So there was only one reason I could think of why she was telling me she had the ring—she must want to help me.

"You met Peter when he was alive," I said. "I don't know if you've ever been in love before, but Peter is my soul mate. I'll never love anyone but him. So I'm asking you—no, I'm *begging* you—for one wish on the ring. Just one. It's all I ask."

"I have been in love before," Mary said slowly. "I've fallen in love many times, although nothing as strong as what you claim to have with Peter. So yes, I'll give you your wish."

"Really?" I asked. "Just like that?"

"Not quite." The words were like a knife to my heart, but she said them so calmly that I didn't lose hope entirely. "I'll do it in exchange for something from you."

I wanted to tell her that I'd do *anything*, but I held my tongue, since saying such a thing could do nothing but get me in trouble.

"What do you want?" I asked instead.

"A future favor," she replied. "Sometime in the future, when I need you do to something for me, I'll let you know. You'll be bound to do as I ask, no matter what."

"I can do that," I said, since it was far from the worst thing she could have requested from me. "As long as you don't ask me to do something crazy, like kill myself."

"I hope you trust my character enough to know that I would never ask you to do such a thing."

"I do," I said, since it was true. Mary had founded the Haven because of her insatiable desire for peace and harmony between kingdoms. She cared about not just supernatural lives, but for human lives, too.

If there was one person I trusted to promise a future favor to and not be unfairly taken advantage of when it was time for me to fulfill that favor, it was the leader of the Haven.

"I'll do it," I said, and with that, she brought out a knife, and we made the blood oath.

39

KARINA

Once the blood oath was made, Mary rubbed the sapphire ring, and out came Geneva.

The witch was dressed in the same black flapper outfit she'd been wearing when Annika had called on her in the throne room of the Vale. But her hair was smushed and her eyes were red—as if she'd been crying.

"What?" She sniffed and rubbed under her nose, glaring at Mary.

I had no idea what was wrong with Geneva, but truthfully, it wasn't my problem. All I cared about was her completing my wish.

"I know I promised to give you space while you grieved." Mary spoke calmly and softly, as if talking to a child. "However, Princess Karina has come to me with a request, and it simply cannot wait."

"Get on with it, then." Geneva crossed her arms and raised her chin, waiting. "Although I'm sure you know that while you wear the ring, I don't have to do anything *she* asks." She tilted her head toward me, scrunching her nose as if I smelled bad.

After my long travel day, I likely did.

"I'm aware," Mary said. "Which is why *I'm* commanding you to bring the love of Karina's life, Peter, back from the dead."

"No can do," Geneva said simply. "I can't bring people back from the dead."

"You can't?" My stomach sunk, and I glared at her, ready to grab the knife from the table and attack. But I controlled myself, since violence wouldn't get me anywhere in the Haven. "Or you *won't*?"

"I can't," she said. "No witch can bring someone back from the dead—not even me. It's beyond our capabilities."

"How do I know you're telling the truth?" She had to be lying. I'd come too far for her not to be able to do this.

"Because I'm bound by the spell on the ring to do anything its owner commands," she said. "If I were able to do it, I'd *have* to do it. Also, you're not the only one who's lost someone you love. If I were able to bring people back from the dead, don't you think I'd have done it by now? Witches can't raise the dead. Trust me, I wish it were otherwise, but it isn't."

"Fine," I said. "No witch can bring Peter back from the dead. But if a witch can't bring someone back ... who *can*?"

Geneva shrugged, looking wistfully back at her ring. She clearly wanted to return there so she could get back to her private little pity party.

She seemed pretty tough, so I assumed that whatever she was crying about had truly shaken her to the core.

"You need to ask her," I said, turning to Mary. "She's not bound to answer me."

"Okay," Mary replied. "Our agreement only allowed for one wish, but I'll give you this exception."

"Thank you." I smiled, grateful to Mary for doing this—and also knowing that if there was ever a way for me to pay her back, I would.

"Who's capable of bringing back the dead?" Mary said, turning to Geneva. "If you know, I command you to answer truthfully."

"The fae," Geneva said immediately.

The moment she said the words, Mary's face paled.

"What's that look for?" I asked, continuing before she could answer. "The fae are impossible to find, aren't they? Or they're all dead?"

In all my time on Earth, I'd never met a fae, nor met anyone who had.

But they could bring Peter back. Which meant if I needed to go to the end of the Earth to find a fae, I would.

"They're not impossible to find, and they're certainly not dead," Mary said, her expression grave. "I know how to find them."

"You'll tell me?" I knew I was asking for another favor, but I was so close to getting Peter back that I could practically feel the warmth of his lips on mine. I couldn't stop pushing now.

"I recommend *against* going to the fae," she began. "You might think they're helping you, but in reality, the fae are always helping themselves. However, I can tell from the look on your face that if I don't tell you, you won't rest until you find someone else who can. So yes, I'll tell you how to find the fae. But whatever the outcome, don't say I didn't warn you."

I simply nodded for her to continue, and from there, she told me everything.

40

ANNIKA

THE MAGES HAD CAST a boundary spell around the boat —it would last until we got past the mist—to keep it a bearable temperature. Jacen had taken the role as captain, and after a few starting difficulties at the wheel, he'd gotten the hang of it.

"I think it's time that I took a turn," I said playfully, somehow managing to be lighthearted despite the challenges I knew we had ahead.

"No need," he said, pressing a few buttons. "I've got it on autopilot. We should be good until we hit the mist."

"Nice," I said. "How'd you figure out how to—"

He grabbed me and kissed me, stopping me mid-sentence.

My heart leaped into my throat, and I kissed him back with all the longing I'd felt since we'd been taken down by the vampires in the woods when he'd been trying to help me escape the Vale. Yes, I'd kissed him since then as Princess Ana, but it wasn't the same.

He pushed me back against the window, and I broke the kiss for a second, wanting to see his face. His eyes were closed, but then he opened them, the intensity of his silver gaze reaching deep into my soul. He was looking at me like I meant the world to him. I had a feeling that I was looking at him in the exact same way, too.

Despite the past few weeks being a total mess, they'd gotten me here, with Jacen. For that, I would always be grateful.

Suddenly I saw a flicker in the corner of my eye.

I turned my head and saw a glowing green light, growing larger with each passing second. There was pink in it as well, swirling together to create a breathtaking show.

"The Northern Lights." I gasped, taking hold of Jacen's hand. "Come on. Let's watch."

He led me to the outside deck, and we snuggled on the bench, watching the incredible display. The lights were science, not magic, but they were more amazing than any magic I'd ever seen.

"Have you ever seen anything so beautiful?" I asked.

"Other than you?" he teased, and I rolled my eyes, nudging him in the side.

"Come on," I said. "I'm serious."

"Me too," he said. "You're more beautiful to me than even the Northern Lights."

His lips found mine once more, and while I enjoyed the kiss, I pulled away again.

"Hey." Mischief crossed his eyes, and he leaned toward me. "I was enjoying that."

"Me too." I smiled to make sure he didn't take it personally and glanced back up at the dancing sky. "But how often do we get to see *this*?"

"Fair point." He wrapped his arm around my shoulders, and together, we took in the spectacle. The bright colors covered every inch of the sky—a dancing neon flame that went on for miles and miles.

We watched the light show in peaceful silence for a few minutes.

Then, my stomach growled.

My cheeks flushed, embarrassed by its loud rumble, and I silently commanded my stomach to be quiet. But it betrayed me, growling again.

Ever since my Nephilim blood had been activated, I'd been hungry a lot more than I'd been as a human.

"We have those sandwiches in the fridge," Jacen said. "Stay here and watch the lights. I'll go get you one."

He returned a few minutes later with a blanket, drinks, and a sandwich. He laid the blanket on the floor and started setting up.

"How do you feel about picnics?" he asked.

"I've never had one," I said. "But I couldn't think of a better first time." I helped him finish setting up, and then dug into the food. I was the only one who ate—he insisted on only having blood. While vampires could enjoy food, they didn't need it to survive, so he refused to dig into our limited food supply.

"This is our first date as *us*," I said once I finished my sandwich. "As Jacen and Annika."

"What about the night we met?" he asked. "When we hung out in the attic of the Tavern."

"That wasn't an official date," I said. "It was the night we met. It's different."

"All right." He smiled. "If that's how it is, then yeah, I suppose this *is* our first date."

And what a perfect first date it was. We snuggled, kissed and talked—all while watching the Northern Lights—eventually falling asleep in each other's arms under the dancing spectacle in the sky.

41

ANNIKA

I awoke with a gasp, unable to breathe.

I was surrounded by white mist, so thick that it was impossible to see. It burned my lungs. They felt like they were on *fire*.

We needed to turn around—now. Get out of here before suffocating to death.

I jolted up to run toward the wheel, but Jacen's hand found mine, stopping me. "Relax," he murmured in my ear. "You'll feel better when you do. The mist is trying to make us want to turn around, but it's not going to hurt us. The more you panic, the worse it'll get."

I recalled the mages saying the same thing before sending us off on the boat. As I thought back their words, I was able to suck in a shallow breath—one after another until my breathing was almost back to normal again. It still hurt, but it was bearable. I was also able to see clearer, too. Not incredibly clear—it looked like a foggy day—but at least everything wasn't whited out anymore.

"Thanks," I told Jacen once I'd gotten ahold of myself.

I thought it would have taken longer before reaching the mist. I'd been planning on checking out the weapons, but then I'd gotten distracted by the Northern Lights—and by Jacen. I'd figured we'd have time to grab them in the morning. But the boat was only protected by the mages boundary until we passed through the mist. Which meant we didn't have much longer until we were vulnerable to anything that might attack.

"We need to get weapons." I stood up and headed toward the storage room.

Jacen was at my side, apparently in agreement with my assessment.

I grabbed the first weapon that called out to me—a long silver sword in a sheath that I could strap around my back. Jacen went for two gleaming knives and sheathed them to his sides.

"You know how to use that?" He motioned to the long-sword that strangely enough, felt more at home than ever on my back.

"No idea." I shrugged. "My instinct pulled me toward it, so I'm hoping that means yes."

"Sounds good enough to me," he said, heading out of the room. "Come on. We should get out there so we're ready once the mist ends."

We headed back up to the steering room. The mist pricked my skin this time, like tiny little needles. It *burned*, but once I relaxed and reminded myself what the mages said about how the mist wouldn't actually hurt us, the pain subsided.

After a few more minutes, the mist got lighter and lighter, and then it faded completely.

Ahead of us was an island, and in the center of the island was a giant, blooming tree. The tree was tall enough that it touched the clouds themselves, and the branches hung so far out that the tips of them reached the end of the island itself. It gleamed with light—not a reflection of the sun, but a light that seemed to glow from within.

"The Tree of Life," I breathed, amazed to be in its presence. Even though I hadn't known about the Tree until recently, the sight of it was holy and intense.

Despite wanting to go full speed ahead, the sun was up, which was going to be a problem. But luckily not for long, since we were so far north that there weren't many hours of sunlight.

"Maybe we should stop," I told Jacen. "Wait for the sun to set. It won't be out for long."

"I'm fine under cover," he said. "And once we get to the island, the branches go far enough out that they'll provide shade."

"Are you sure?" I asked.

His only response was to press harder on the gas pedal, urging the boat faster to shore.

Suddenly, something thumped on the side of the boat.

I looked back in panic, but nothing was there.

"What was that?" Jacen asked, still focused straight ahead.

"I don't—" I was cut off by another thump, this one so forceful that it caught me off guard and sent me tumbling into the wall.

The engine cut off, and the boat stalled.

"Damn it." Jacen pounded the steering wheel and pressed harder on the gas. When nothing happened, he swiveled around and marched out of the control room, apparently going to figure out what was going on.

I followed him, since there was no way I was letting him go out alone. He shouldn't be going out there at *all*, given the sunlight—but I doubted anything I said would stop him, so I might as well join him.

It didn't take long to see the engine—or rather, what was *left* of the engine. It hung crookedly off the end of the boat, looking like it had been beaten with a sledgehammer.

I didn't know much about boat engines, but it looked past the point of repair.

Jacen glanced over the side of the boat—I assumed to try and figure out what had done that to the engine—and his face fell.

"What is it?" I asked, although I saw the answer a second later.

Beneath the water was the shadow of what could only be a giant, eel-like sea creature. It went so far out in both directions that it seemed like it wrapped around the entire island. It was moving, and while it was underwater right now, I had a feeling it wouldn't stay that way for long. Especially after what it had already done to our engine.

"There were some paddles in the storage room," I said. "I'll go get them."

I doubted that paddling would get us anywhere fast, but Jacen and I were stronger than the average human, so that had to count for something. I hurried to the storage room, grabbed two of the paddles that were hanging next to some life vests on the wall, and ran back up to the deck.

I got there just as something large and slimy

emerged from the water like a serpent—the creature's head.

It looked like an alligator head, with a long snout, scaly skin, and beady eyes—but blown up to the size of a golf cart. Bearing down on us, it rumbled and opened its mouth, revealing rows of teeth like jagged nails.

Jacen was on it in a second, avoiding its mouth while using his knives to slash at its skin. But the skin was hard—so hard that his knives didn't seem to be doing anything at all.

I hurried to join him, dropping the paddles and reaching for my sword. I aimed for the creature's skin, but like the knives, my sword bounced right off. It was like its skin was made of metal.

Jacen reeled back his arm and threw one of his knives at the creature, landing right in the center of one of its eyes.

The creature screamed in pain, and I thrust my sword forward, aiming for the softer, more vulnerable flesh inside its mouth. I nicked its cheek, but quickly pulled my sword back, not wanting it to get caught in the creature's mouth.

Then Jacen threw his second knife, and it hit the creature's other eye, blinding it. The hilts of both knives stuck out where its eyes had been.

"Score," I said at the same time as it opened its mouth

to scream again. I used the opportunity to go at it again with my sword, digging deeper this time. If I could just get through the roof of its mouth, then I could go straight through its brain…

But the creature jerked its head up, its teeth clanging against my sword—and my wrist—sending the weapon to the other side of the boat.

I pulled my arm back and cried out in pain.

The tooth had gone straight through my wrist. It must have hit a vein, because blood was everywhere—*my* blood.

"Watch out!" Jacen yelled as the creature lunged forward, and he threw himself at me to push me out of the way.

I toppled to the ground, turning around just in time to see the creature's jaw crunch down on Jacen's legs.

"No!" I yelled, watching as the creature pulled back, as if to drag Jacen out to sea. But Jacen grabbed onto the side of the boat, holding on for dear life.

If the creature didn't open its mouth, Jacen was going to die.

In a split-second decision, I ran for the paddles, grabbed them, and shoved the narrow ends straight into the creature's nostrils. I shoved them in real deep—deep enough that they were wedged halfway inside there.

The ends of the paddles were drenched in the blood

that was still pouring from my wrists, and spots danced in front of my eyes from the blood loss.

The wound was healing, but not fast enough. To make things even worse, at some point during the fight, the creature had bit a hole straight through the boat. We were taking on water—slowly—but it didn't look good.

Hopelessness descended upon me, but then the creature opened its mouth, just like I'd wanted it to.

The ends of the paddles had blocked air from entering its nasal passages, giving it only one way to get in air—its mouth. As it took a breath, I snapped back into focus, grabbing Jacen's arms and pulling him inside the boat.

His legs were bloodied, mangled messes—I couldn't look at them without wincing in pain. There was no way he could stand, let alone fight.

But the creature was still there, and it was coming down again. I couldn't get to my sword in time, and trying to get one of the knives embedded in the creature's eyes would be near impossible.

If I didn't try *something*, this monster was going to kill us both. So I used my uninjured arm to reach for my only remaining weapon—Laila's stake that I'd been keeping strapped to my side—and threw it into the roof of the creature's mouth, straight up into its brain.

The creature's head snapped back, and it crashed back into the sea.

The water was still leaking into the boat, but other than that, all was silent for the first time since we'd come through the mist.

I hugged my wounded wrist to my chest, putting pressure on it to stop the bleeding. It seemed to be helping. The hole was knitting together, but I'd lost so much blood that I was sitting in a puddle of it.

I used my last bit of energy to glance over at Jacen and make sure his wounds were healing, and then everything went dark.

42

KARINA

MARY HAD REFUSED to allow a witch of the Haven to transport me to Ireland. My going to the fae had nothing to do with creating peace between kingdoms, so it wasn't the Haven's obligation to give me a ride there. And since Mary had already gone beyond what I'd asked of her by telling me how to summon the fae, I wasn't going to push it.

Unfortunately, that meant flying commercial—again. This airport wasn't as crowded, since I guessed winter wasn't a popular time to visit Ireland. The taxi line wasn't terribly long, but each second wasted was one more second I could have with Peter. So I sauntered to the front of the line and used compulsion to get the next taxi, just like I'd done in India.

The car reeked of alcohol, which I supposed must be

somewhat typical for a cab in Ireland. How many drunken partiers must the driver have taken home after the bars closed?

Luckily, this driver was nice enough to stop and wait for me while I walked into a store for supplies. For a charge, of course—although little did he know that I had no intention of paying that charge.

I hopped back into the waiting taxi, smiling and placing my bag of equipment by my side. It was a long drive to where we were heading, and I stayed quiet the entire time, unwilling to participate in any chitchat.

The less I knew about this man, the better.

We finally arrived, and just like before, I used the moment after he requested payment to take a drink from his throat.

This man's blood tasted slightly sour, like he'd recently had beer.

Blood never tasted as good when the human had been drinking alcohol.

But that wasn't what concerned me. No—I was more concerned with how many lives this man had endangered by drinking while working. I doubted this was the first time he'd done this. One thing I'd learned in all my years was that when someone was acting a certain way, it was usually because it was a habit.

Someday, this man was going to get someone killed.

At least the fact that he was drinking and driving would help curb the guilt of what I needed to do next.

Because there was still one last ingredient I needed to call upon the fae—the blood of a human I'd killed with my own hand.

Once I'd had my fill, I pulled away, licking the remaining blood from my lips and watching as the wound sealed closed. The man was still blinking away the haze of the venom when I reached for my newly acquired knife and slashed it across his pale, fleshy throat.

The cut was so deep that he couldn't even scream.

Guilt wracked my chest, but I only had to think Peter's name to push the unwelcome feeling away. If this man had to die for Peter to live, then so be it.

"Don't move," I said with compulsion, reaching for the other item I'd purchased—a plastic Tupperware container.

I held it under the man's neck, tipping him forward so the blood flowed into the container. I let it fill until there was no blood left to drain—far past the point when his heart stopped beating.

"Thank you." I placed the lid on the container, sealing it to make sure it was tight. "I'll make sure your sacrifice wasn't in vain."

Then I put the car in neutral and rolled it into the forest.

The man would be found, eventually.

By then, I'd be long gone—and Peter and I would finally be together again.

43

KARINA

I FOLLOWED the directions Mary had given me, and it wasn't long until I arrived to the mystical garden of the fae.

Despite the majority of Ireland being dead and covered in snow in the height of winter, this garden was green and alive, with a sparkling pond in the center. It was like stepping into a bubble of summer. But that wasn't what surprised me about it.

What surprised me was that I wasn't the only one there.

A young girl in a short, green dress sat perched on a rock. She reminded me of Tinkerbell, but full sized—and without the wings.

Her lips turned up into a small smile when she saw

me. "Hello, Karina" she said calmly. "I've been waiting for you."

I didn't move toward her, not wanting to startle her. Also—while I hated to admit it—I was slightly spooked. The girl didn't look older than ten, yet she spoke like an adult.

"Who are you?" I asked. "And how do you know my name?"

"My name is Fiona," she said. "I know your name because a friend told me you would be here. I've been quite anxious for your arrival." She paused, patting the rock next to her. "Sit down and join me. We have so much to discuss."

I took a deep breath and did as she'd asked, since this was why I was here—to meet with the fae. I'd never met a fae before, but this girl seemed to fit all of the qualifications for being one. Still, it was better safe than sorry.

"Are you a fae?" I asked, doing my best to make myself comfortable on the rock. It was a bit difficult, since it was lumpy to sit on. I placed my pack and container of blood on the ground, but kept my knife in its place in my boot.

No matter *what* this girl was—a fae or some other type of supernatural—I couldn't let my guard down.

"I am." She giggled, sounding like a little girl for the

first time since I'd arrived. "Although I understand why you're wary. This is hardly the typical way my kind operate."

"No," I agreed. "I'd been told I needed to wait for the full moon, and *then* come here to call on you."

"Yet the moon isn't full," she said.

"I know." I glanced up at the silver crescent gleaming in the sky. "But I was going to try anyway, just in case it were possible to call on you during other times, too."

"Interesting." She tilted her head, studying me. "It's true that we can only journey to Earth from the Otherworld on the nights of the full moon. However, a dear friend of mine has the ability of omniscient sight. He was called to Earth on the most recent full moon, and while here, he had a vision that you would come here before the next full moon—and that you would have something I desired. He owed me a favor, so he told me of his vision… and now I'm here." She smiled and shrugged, as if it were as simple as that.

"Wow," I said. "So you've been waiting here for me for days?"

"I have," she said. "Although when you're immortal, a few days hardly feel like much time, do they?"

I nodded, although I had a sneaking suspicion that she'd seen many more centuries than I.

"My friend also told me that if I waited until the next full moon to see you, it would be too late," she added.

"What does that mean?" I shifted in place, not liking the sound of that.

"I don't know." She giggled again, and the hairs on my arms prickled. "But it hardly matters, because you're here now. So let's get down to business, shall we?"

"Okay," I said. "I came here because—"

"You're jumping ahead of yourself," she interrupted, holding a hand in the air to stop me. "We have yet to discuss your payment for my passage to Earth."

"I never officially called you here." I glanced at the container of blood, guilty that I'd ended up killing that man for no reason.

Although... maybe it *hadn't* been for no reason.

I picked up the container and held it out to Fiona. "Will this human blood be sufficient payment?" I asked. "I brought it here specifically for you."

She swatted it out of my hand, and it hit the ground with so much force that it split open, the blood leaking out and soaking into the ground.

"The fae do not crave blood as vampires do." She scrunched her nose, as if vampires disgusted her. "I mean no offense, of course," she added with an innocent smile.

"None taken." I sat straighter, thinking of only one thing—Peter's return. His coming back was worth keeping my cool with this petulant fae girl. "Since you don't want the blood, what *do* you want?"

"As payment for my passage to Earth, I'd like the portrait you carry with you." She looked to my bag and lit up gleefully. "The one of your true love."

I jerked back, shocked by her request. "Why do you want a faded old portrait?" I asked, truly confused about her reasoning.

"That object is more than just a portrait." She focused on me again, her eyes gleaming with desire. "I can feel its energy from here. You've carried it with you for so long that you've imprinted some of your most intense emotions upon it, making it quite valuable indeed. Surely it's worth giving up?" She brushed off her skirt and moved forward on the rock, as if preparing to stand. "If not, I'll be on my way."

Ache filled my heart at the thought of giving up my most treasured possession.

But that's all the portrait was—a possession. I'd give it up ten fold to have Peter alive and well.

"Wait," I said, and she smirked, situating herself again.

She tilted her head, clearly waiting.

My hands trembled as I unzipped the bag and pulled out Peter's portrait, flipping it over to take one final look at his soulful eyes.

This is for you, Peter, I thought as I handed it to Fiona.

44

KARINA

Fiona held the portrait to her heart and closed her eyes, a mask of calm transforming her features. "Lovely," she said, opening her eyes again and placing the portrait in her pocket. "Now that *that's* settled, we can move forward with our discussion. So tell me, Karina—why do you seek my help?"

"Peter—the man in the portrait—died many years ago," I began, glancing toward where the portrait now lay in her pocket. "I want you to bring him back, just as he was before his death, but fully intact and healed. I want his return to be permanent."

I needed to be careful in my wording—the fae couldn't lie, but they were notoriously tricky creatures when it came to making deals.

"I cannot provide him god-like immortality," she

said. "Every creature—even the fae—has an Achilles heel."

"But you can bring him back?" I sat forward, more hopeful than ever.

"I can." She nodded. "But first, I must ask—what do you know of the fae?"

"Not much," I admitted. "Just that you're immortal, you live in the Otherworld, and that you rarely come to Earth."

"That's correct," she said. "Each of us also has a different magical ability—some more rare and powerful than others."

"Interesting," I said, since she was correct—I hadn't known that. What she'd said earlier about her friend with omniscient sight now made more sense. "What's your magical ability?"

"I'm glad you asked." She straightened her shoulders and smiled, smoothing out her dress. "I'm a traveler fae. Traveler fae are extremely rare fae who can travel into the Beyond—the place where the creatures of all realms go when they die. Most traveler fae can only visit the Beyond, but my powers are far stronger than that. It takes a great amount of energy, but I'm also able to bring those in the Beyond back to the world of the living."

"You'll do that?" I was breathless, my heart pounding

with the realization that this was more than just a dream—it was truly possible. "You'll bring Peter back to me?"

"I will." She smiled. "For a price."

Of course—I'd expected as much. "What do you want?" I asked.

"Your memories," she said simply.

I blinked, stunned by her request. "What?" I asked, despite having heard her loud and clear.

"I'd like your memories," she repeated. "All of them."

"I can't give away all of my memories." Horror filled my body at the thought of doing such a thing. "If I did, what would be left of me?"

"Others before you have traded as much," she said. "But I agree—it's a high price to pay, and I'm not so cruel as to strip you of all your memories. A portion of them will do just fine."

"What portion of them?" I was on guard, my stomach twisting with the feeling that she had some kind of terrible trick up her sleeve.

"Just a small portion, in comparison to the time you've lived on Earth." She widened her eyes in a chilling display of innocence. "The only memories of yours I want are the ones you have of Peter."

45

KARINA

"No." I jolted back at her request. "That's not fair."

"The fae don't operate on 'fair.'" Fiona smiled again, but this time it radiated pure maliciousness. "I'm the *only* living fae able to bring souls from the Beyond back to the lands of the living. Now I'm offering to bring back your Peter in exchange for all your memories of him. That's my final offer—do you want to take it or leave it?"

I wanted to tell her absolutely not.

But I held my tongue, giving myself time to think. This was my *one* chance to get Peter back—she'd said so herself, and the fae couldn't lie.

If I said no, I would never see Peter again. At least, not until I died and passed into the Beyond—and who knew how long that would be?

I'd take my own life to join him in the Beyond, but I'd learned from a young age that those who took their own lives ended up in Hell.

If I woke up in Hell, then I'd *never* see Peter again.

"There's nothing else you want?" I tried, although a sinking feeling told me it was hopeless.

"No," she said. "That was my final offer. But if you don't think you'll fall in love with Peter again without your prior memories of him, then I suppose it's not worth it for you to take me up on this deal, is it?"

I seethed at her implication that I wouldn't love Peter if it weren't for our memories together. Peter and I were soul mates. I'd known we were meant to be together when I'd first seen him on the deck of the *Olympic*, his coat flapping in the wind as he'd gazed out over the ocean.

Even if my memories of him were stripped away, I'd fall in love with him all over again the moment I saw him. I was absolutely sure of it.

"He'll still have his memories of me," I said. "Correct?"

"He'll retain all his Earthly memories," she said. "He made no deal with me, so they will remain as they were."

I nodded, glad that if anything, we'd at least have that.

Once Peter and I were reunited, he'd fill me in on all

I'd forgotten. Perhaps hearing of our memories from his lips would cause my memories of him to return.

If it didn't, we'd form new memories—together.

"All right." I met Fiona's hollow eyes, resolved in my decision. "I accept your deal."

46

KARINA

"Perfect." Fiona rubbed her hands together in excitement. "It'll take me a few hours to travel to the Beyond, retrieve your Peter, and bring him back here. But first—we must finalize our deal."

She placed her fingers on my temples, and a pleasant buzz tore through my body, followed by a surprising feeling of emptiness.

"All done," she said, and then she vanished into thin air.

My head felt light and heavy at the same time—like I'd had too many glasses of champagne—and I gazed around the faerie garden, confused about what had just happened.

I'd been talking with the fae named Fiona—I'd made some kind of deal with her. Then she'd done something to me. I could feel it... although I couldn't pinpoint what exactly *it* was.

What deal had I made? Why had I come here at all?

I pressed my hand to my forehead and contemplated the past few weeks, willing it to make sense.

King Nicolae and I had made a deal. I'd go to the Vale under the pretense of seeking Prince Jacen's hand in marriage—but that wasn't truly why I'd gone.

The king had wanted the Vale to fall because he wanted Queen Laila to be his. In return, he'd promised me Geneva's sapphire ring.

I'd wanted the ring—who *didn't* want a ring that contained the most powerful witch in the world, who could grant you any wish your heart desired? Of course I'd said yes.

To help the Vale fall, I'd worked with the wolves.

I'd met Noah.

My heart fluttered at the thought of his name.

It was hard to believe that I'd been so disgusted by wolves before meeting him. In our time working together, Noah had trusted me more than any man I'd ever known. I'd trusted him, too.

I'd trusted Noah so much that once the Nephilim girl had revealed herself and killed the queen, I'd left the palace and run straight to him. Just the memory of the way his kind eyes had watched me every time we were together made my heart warm.

I was falling in love with Noah—I was likely already there.

But my time with him had been too short. After running to the camp, I'd gone straight to the Haven to retrieve Geneva's sapphire ring.

The ring was the only thing that could get me what I wanted.

What had I wanted?

I ran my fingers through my hair, frustrated that the answer wasn't there. It was at the tip of my tongue, but at the same time, it was gone. Out of reach and impossible to touch.

I must have wanted to help the wolves of the Vale. Their Savior was rising soon—He was going to bring them peace and prosperity. Noah and all the other wolves in the Vale deserved peace after all the years the packs had been at war.

Now that Laila was dead, King Nicolae would surely banish me from the Carpathian Kingdom forever.

Which meant Noah—and the pack—was the closest thing to family I would have left.

I must have made some kind of deal with the fae to help the wolves. I just wished I could remember *what* deal I'd made.

I paced around, frustrated when the answer continued to evade me.

Finally, I dropped my arms to my sides, giving up. Noah would help me. I *knew* he would help me. And next time I saw him, I wasn't going to hide from my feelings anymore. Time was too precious—with war on the horizon, we had no idea how much of it we had left.

And so, I picked up my pack of cash and left the faerie garden behind, eager to return to the Vale and tell Noah my true feelings for him once and for all.

47

PETER

I SUCKED IN A DEEP BREATH, the air burning my lungs as if I hadn't breathed in decades.

The sky was dark, although the first rays of light were starting to stream through the clouds. I was laying on something soft, squishy, and covered in dew—grass. The air smelled fresh and clean. Forest animals chirped nearby, and I heard a light splashing of water.

I sat up and looked around the strange garden blooming in the midst of winter, my mind muddled in confusion.

The last thing I remembered were the wolves storming the castle, and the other vampires of the Carpathian Kingdom and I uniting to stop them from entering. The Nephilim had gotten the wolves to do their dirty work of breaking into the castle, and if the wolves won, the Nephilim would follow in their wake.

We'd *had* to hold them off.

I remembered fighting with Karina by my side—she was so beautiful in battle. Delicate, graceful, and lethal, like a snake. I was always glad I was fighting with her and not against her.

We'd *always* fight together. We were soul mates—two parts of a single whole.

But that fight had been different than the others—it had been more frantic… more *desperate*. I'd glanced at Karina to make sure she was all right, and then there'd been an explosive pain in my chest.

After that, I remembered nothing.

Had Karina survived? Did the wolves beat us? Where was I now? How did I get here?

I had so many questions, and I knew the answers to none. But if I were alive, that had to be a good thing. The Nephilim must not have won.

If they'd won, they would have killed every last vampire in the castle.

A soft breeze blew through the clearing, and I was overtaken with the sudden scent of blood. The blood smelled dead—like it had been sitting out for hours—but I was so starving that even stale blood made my fangs emerge.

I hurried to the scent and grabbed a strange plastic container, pouring the blood that was left of it into my mouth and licking the inside clean. The blood was tainted with alcohol, but I was too hungry to be picky.

I felt like I hadn't had a drink in forever. And that small bit hadn't been enough—I needed more.

But wherever I was, the sun was rising and there was no sign of any humans nearby for me to drink from.

I was too weak to tolerate direct sunlight for long. So I situated myself under a tree—a comfortable spot where I could wait for the day to pass.

Once night fell, I would leave this place and go home to the Carpathian Kingdom, which was where I would find the home of my heart—Karina.

I hope you enjoyed The Vampire Fate! If so, I'd love if you left a review. Reviews help readers find the book, and I read each and every one of them :)

Reviews for the first book in the series are the most helpful. Here's the link on Amazon where you can leave your review ➜ The Vampire Wish

The final book in the series, The Vampire War, is out now!

Get your copy now at:
mybook.to/vampirewar

You can also check out the cover and description for The Vampire War below. (You may need to turn the page to view the cover and description.)

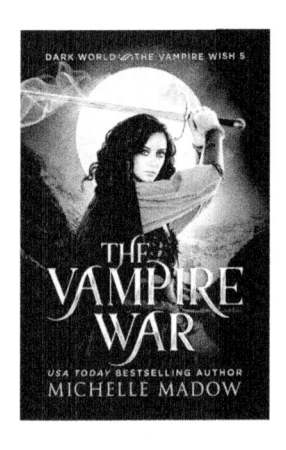

Find the Holy Grail. Win the war. Save the world.

A lot has changed for Annika since being kidnapped by vampires to become a blood slave in their hidden kingdom of the Vale. Not only has she learned she's a Nephilim—a race that's supposedly extinct—but she's found herself on a dangerous quest for the Holy Grail. Luckily, she has the vampire Prince Jacen by her side, and the two of them feel ready for anything—especially now that they trust each other more than ever.

But finding the Grail is only the beginning. Because when Annika learns that a demon is leading a pack of wolves to war against the vampires, she *must* stop him before it's too late. If she can't, he'll open a Gate to Hell… and the world as she knows it will be lost forever.

Get ready for an action-packed, adventure-filled ride in the EPIC season finale of The Vampire Wish series!

Get your copy now at:
mybook.to/vampirewar

Also, make sure you never miss a new release by signing up to get emails and/or texts when my books come out!

Sign up for emails: michellemadow.com/subscribe

Sign up for texts: michellemadow.com/texts

And if you want to hang out with me and other readers of my books, make sure to join my Facebook group: https://www.facebook.com/groups/michellemadow

Thanks for reading my books, and I look forward to chatting with you!

ABOUT THE AUTHOR

Michelle Madow is a USA Today bestselling author of fast-paced, young adult fantasy novels that will leave you turning the pages wanting more! Her books are full of magic, adventure, romance, and twists you'll never see coming.

Michelle grew up in Maryland, and now lives in Florida. She's loved reading for as long as she can remember. She wrote her first book in her junior year of college and hasn't stopped writing since! She also loves traveling, and has been to all seven continents. Someday, she hopes to travel the world for a year on a cruise ship.

Visit author.to/MichelleMadow to view a full list of Michelle's novels on Amazon.

THE VAMPIRE FATE

Published by Dreamscape Publishing

Copyright © 2017 Michelle Madow

This book is a work of fiction. Though some actual towns, cities, and locations may be mentioned, they are used in a fictitious manner and the events and occurrences were invented in the mind and imagination of the author. Any similarities of characters or names used within to any person past, present, or future is coincidental.

All rights reserved. No part of this book may be used or reproduced in any manner whatsoever without written permission from the author. Brief quotations may be embodied in critical articles or reviews.

❀ Created with Vellum

Printed in Great Britain
by Amazon